W9-ARL-674

His Hands Closed On Her Waist...

...and she couldn't move.

The moment she pressed against him she was lost. She wanted Jake's kiss despite the anger that flared up at reminders of the past. At that moment she couldn't move away if her life depended on it.

"Damn, Madison," he whispered, right before his mouth came down on hers.

She kissed him back as if she'd been waiting for this moment since the night he'd walked out. Her flesh ached for his touch. The anger, the pain and the memories were replaced by desire...until she realized what she was doing.

She broke away, gasping for breath. "I never meant for that to happen."

She was torn between wanting him and hating her loss of control. She'd thought she was over wanting him, beyond responding to him.

With one kiss he'd shattered that illusion.

* * *

The Texan's Forbidden Fiancée is part of the Lone Star Legends series from *USA TODAY* bestselling author Sara Orwig.

* * *

If you're on Twitter, tell us what you think of Harlequin Desire! #harlequindesire

Dear Reader,

The inspiration for my Lone Star Legends stories, beginning with *The Texan's Forbidden Fiancée,* came from growing up listening to my relatives tell stories and legends from past generations. Every area seems to have its own legends, myths and stories passed down through families. So here is a Texas legend of buried treasure, ancestors killed in a feud who were buried where they died and a secret treasure that a handsome Texas rancher, Jake Calhoun, seeks when he asks to search his neighbor's land. His request is complicated by his past with his beautiful blonde neighbor, because years earlier he'd disappeared out of her life without explanation on their wedding day.

This book starts a series involving the Milans and the Calhouns, two families with generations of feuding, brought together by love, yet some still not able to stop the hatred even though legends change their lives. Our history still influences our present, and this is the beginning story of families whose lives are changed by their legends handed down through the years.

Best wishes,

Sara Orwig

THE TEXAN'S
FORBIDDEN FIANCÉE

—

SARA ORWIG

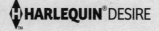
HARLEQUIN® DESIRE

Recycling programs
for this product may
not exist in your area.

ISBN-13: 978-0-373-73321-7

THE TEXAN'S FORBIDDEN FIANCÉE

Printed in U.S.A.

Books by Sara Orwig

Harlequin Desire

Silhouette Desire

Other titles by this author
available in ebook format.

SARA ORWIG

lives in Oklahoma. She has a patient husband who will take her on research trips anywhere, from big cities to old forts. She is an avid collector of Western history books. With a master's degree in English, Sara has written historical romance, mainstream fiction and contemporary romance. Books are beloved treasures that take Sara to magical worlds, and she loves both reading and writing them.

With thanks to Stacy Boyd,
Allison Carroll and Maureen Walters.
And with love to David and all my family.

One

In the small town of Verity, Texas, when the door to the Texas United Western Bank opened, Jake Calhoun's breath whooshed out as if a fist slammed into his gut. Through the years he had imagined this moment, yet he had thought it would never take place. Now every vivid detail became etched in his memory.

Across the street Madison Milan stepped into the September morning sunlight and glanced around. Sunshine glinted on her thick brown hair that was pulled back and tied with a red scarf. Dressed in jeans, a red shirt showing beneath her open denim jacket, with loafers on her feet, she answered a greeting of someone who passed her.

The shock of finally seeing her rocked him. She was not a figment of his imagination. She was real, alive and only two hundred yards away. Anger surged in his bloodstream, swiftly replaced by desire, intense, hot and startling. Gone was the momentary jolt of finally facing her, replaced by scalding memories. How could he feel desire? The hurt had been so deep, and so long ago.

The memories bombarded him, quick and relentless. She was the most fun female in the junior class, the prettiest football queen ever and had the best-looking legs of any Verity High cheerleader. But now that girl was gone. In her place stood a beautiful woman. Everyone who passed her on the street acknowledged her and she responded with a smile; some stopped to talk. He wondered if she had such a constant stream of people greeting her every time she came to town. Right now a tall, thin cowboy took his turn chatting with her and she smiled up at him.

Jake's emotions warred over the conflicts that rocked him. On the one hand, he wanted to take her family ranch from her and destroy her. After all, she was a Milan, as deceptive, deceitful and out for Calhoun blood as any other Milan in her family. At the same time, she was beautiful, sexy and the most desirable woman he had ever known.

She had been only a girl when he had gotten the closest to her. They had met in high school and the attraction had been hot and instant. He'd been the quarterback of the football team and she'd been a cheerleader.

His unwanted longing grew stronger, stirred by memories that made him weak in the knees. Memories of her soft lips and hot kisses, her silky hair that hung to her waist then, her laughter and boundless energy, her soft curves against him when they danced. The lightning flashes of memory continued to pound him: how they each fought the attraction because of the feud that raged between their families; their first kiss; the first time they made love— the first for her ever. The recollections were so vivid they seemed recent instead of thirteen years ago. She had married the year she had graduated from college and the union had lasted two months. Since that time she had remained single—he knew that much about her—and it was long enough ago to be significant now.

She was probably as competitive in business now as she had been years ago in sports.

He brought himself back to the problem at hand. He wanted to talk to her, but he hadn't figured on a steady stream of locals who paused to chat with her.

From the background information his staff had put together he knew she usually drove a white four-door pickup to town. He'd spotted it two blocks farther west down Main Street in front of the grocery, and now he wondered if he should wait at the truck for her.

When she turned to walk in that direction, he crossed the street, lengthened his stride until he was half a block behind her. She entered the hardware store and he followed her inside. In minutes he found her in front of the paint section. As he approached her, his pulse quickened.

Madison Milan selected tubes of paint for her next art project, searching for the perfect shade of burnt umber. Out of the corner of her eye, she saw someone moving along the aisle toward her. When she saw who it was, she froze. Her heart missed a beat and then thudded. Anger swept over her, an intense, scorching fury that shocked her because she had convinced herself she had gotten over the past. This was the drawback about moving to the ranch after her parents gave it to her. She had come every fall and late spring for the past three years, being careful to avoid Verity as much as possible just to avoid running into Jake. This was the moment she had hoped would never happen. At the same time, an unwanted streak of desire heightened her fury. She didn't want to feel desire when she encountered Jake Calhoun.

He had grown taller. His shoulders appeared broader.

He had filled out and he was even more handsome. He wasn't the nineteen-year-old boy she remembered.

How had he found her? She hadn't noticed him on the street. Or was this coincidence? She didn't think it was.

He stopped only feet away and she hoped he couldn't hear her pounding heart.

"'Hello' seems a little ridiculous," he said, his voice deeper than she recalled.

"'Goodbye' is sufficient. I don't care to talk to you or anyone from your company about drilling on Milan land. I don't care to talk to any Calhoun. End of discussion."

She started to turn away and he placed his fingers lightly on her forearm. It was a feather touch, barely discernible, certainly not actually detaining her, but she stopped instantly and a current sizzled from that faint contact. She stood immobile, bound by a nonexistent hold and intense dark brown eyes.

"It isn't about drilling."

"You're not dredging up the past, are you? I definitely don't want to hear about that."

"No, I'm not," he said, suddenly looking hard, angry and withdrawn. A muscle worked in his jaw. His reaction startled her because she was the injured party, not Jake. Why was he angry? Instantly she blocked the question. She didn't want to know what he thought or felt about that time in their lives. She tried to focus and pay attention as he continued.

"This isn't the place to talk, but…it's about a shoot-out between our families long ago on your land and the old legend of buried treasure. I think you'll be interested, so at least listen and don't miss out on something we both might want."

Surprised, skeptical, she suspected he was fabricating a tale about the ancient incident as an excuse to talk to her and to get on her land. It would be another deceptive Calhoun trick to steal something from a Milan. Their families had been feuding since their first respective ancestors had settled here in the days after the Civil War. She didn't figure the feud would end with them.

"I don't believe you and I don't trust you," she said, barely able to speak above a whisper and sounding unconvincing even to herself. How could he turn her to mush by his mere presence and one look from his dark eyes?

"Madison, at least listen and then make your decision. This is important. Let's meet where we won't be constantly interrupted. Come to dinner at my ranch. Or let me take you to Dallas to dinner. Whatever you want. Just somewhere quiet and private and on neutral ground. This concerns your family, too."

"Hi, Jake," a female voice behind him said as if giving emphasis to his request. He turned slightly and faced another local.

"Hi, Becky," he said, greeting a friend he had known since sixth grade.

Becky Worthington smiled broadly, looking back and forth between them and then focusing on Jake and stepping closer to him. "Nice to see you. You don't come into town often, do you?"

"No, I'm rarely at the ranch because I'm in Dallas a lot of the time and traveling some of the time."

"You should come to town and see people once in a while. Stop in and say hey. I still work at TBC bank, which, of course, I think is the best bank in town," she said, giggling.

"I'll try," Jake stated.

Becky looked back and forth between them. "I didn't mean to interrupt," she said and disappeared around the corner of the aisle from the direction she had come.

When she was out of earshot, Madison resumed their conversation. "An evening out with you? I don't really think so. Everything has been said between us that can be said."

"Far, far from it. You should hear me out. You'll be surprised, Madison. If you're not, tell me and I'll stop talking and go."

She could feel the clash of wills as she shook her head. "Whatever ploy this is, I'm sure a Calhoun itching to drill on Milan land is behind it."

"I want that, too, but it has nothing to do with this. I'm after something else and I think you'll be interested to know about this, too."

"If that's the case, tell me now."

He shook his head. "This is not the place. We were just interrupted, and we will be again. And anyone standing in the next aisle can overhear us. I don't want that and I don't think you will, either. Just go to dinner with me. It's not that big a deal. I can take you home whenever you want."

"Eating out around here won't be one degree better than talking here."

"We won't eat in Verity. We'll fly to Dallas and get a private corner. We won't see people we know. We won't be overheard. I'll bring you home whenever you say. Just trust me, you will not regret listening to me."

Debating what to do, she stared at him. There was no way a Milan could trust a Calhoun—that had been proven to her in a devastating way. She couldn't imagine one thing he could want except to make a pitch to let him drill on her land and she was not going to do that no matter what he said or offered. She couldn't think of another reason he'd want to talk to her. Yet, surely he knew better than to tell her he had another reason and then talk about leasing land. Dinner would be over before it started. But she had to admit she was intrigued. What did he know that she didn't that concerned her ranch?

"All right, Jake. This better be good."

"Spending an evening with me is that bad?" he asked without a change of expression, reinforcing her opinion that he could be highly deceptive.

"I'm equally shocked you want to spend any time with me."

"This will be good, Madison. I'll come by to get you a little before seven Sunday night. Thanks. Absolutely no talk about drilling. I promise."

"I know how much your promise is worth," she couldn't keep from saying. She saw the flicker in his eyes and saw that hardness return to his expression, puzzling her. She turned her back on him and walked away, aiming to complete her purchases and get away from him.

She had intended to get two small brushes, but she wanted out of the store away from Jake more than she wanted the brushes. She had tried to put him and the past out of her thoughts, to stop remembering or hurting. She wished she could have faced him without any reaction instead of this heart-pounding longing. She wished the memories hadn't tumbled back into her thoughts as clearly as if they had parted months ago rather than over a decade ago. Instead, seeing him caused all the old pain and anger to return, as well as the intense physical reaction. He was still the best-looking man she knew. In spite of her hurt and fury, he still set her heart racing.

Suddenly she wanted to go back and cancel the evening with him. Her art career had succeeded beyond all her hopes and expectations. She was constantly busy with what she loved to do. She had remained single because there had been so little time for her personal life and her brief marriage had been disastrous from the first moment. Jake, she knew, was still single, which didn't surprise her. He wasn't the marrying type.

She didn't want to spend a whole evening feeling the way she did now—hurting, drowning in memories of a wedding day that never happened. Memories tore at her heart and fueled an ever-simmering rage when she thought about him. She didn't trust him in the slightest. For a little over one year in her life she had gone against all her family's warnings about the unscrupulous Calhouns and she had trusted Jake. Because of that mistake, he had broken her heart. One thing was certain—no matter what excuses Jake presented, she would never let him drill on Milan land.

She hurried out of the store, striding quickly to her truck, planning to forgo her grocery shopping. She wanted to go home to the Double M Ranch, away from town and any chance of encountering him again. She had been careful, coming to town only once a month, usually getting someone else to pick up groceries and supplies. She would go back to that routine. How she wished she could just as easily obliterate all memories of Jake Calhoun.

Instead, the memories poured over her in a deluge. Growing up, because of the century-and-a-half-old family feud, she never spoke to any Calhouns, but she had been aware of Jake from her first year in high school. They were three years apart in age, but two years in school because she had been tutored at home on the ranch when she was little and when she had started school they'd placed her in the fourth grade instead of the third.

Her first close encounter with Jake had been at a school party in the gym to get everyone acquainted. For one of the dances they had two large circles of kids—boys in the outside ring, girls on the inside. They walked in a circle to a drumbeat until the band began to play, then the boy and girl facing each other danced until the music stopped and everybody resumed walking in a circle to get a new partner.

When the music started, she had been facing Jake. "No. Not a Calhoun," she had said loudly enough for him and everyone around her to hear. She had stepped close to the boy next to him, leaving Jake to the girl next to her. Everyone knew about the feud, and besides, the girl had been a friend and hadn't cared because Jake Calhoun was older, on the football team, well-known and popular.

The next time he passed her at school he walked up close and said, "Thanks for changing partners so I didn't have to." Madison had just continued on her way, wondering if he really would have grabbed a different girl in front of all the other kids. The rest of her freshman year she had never spoken to him again and he didn't speak to her, but she noticed him and he always glanced at her. She had thought it was a pity he was a Calhoun because he was the best-looking boy in the high school.

In her sophomore year, she became a cheerleader. At a game, Jake had come out and was headed to the bench on the sidelines where she had been standing.

"Hi, snooty Miss Milan," he said quietly without even looking at her as he passed her.

She had turned to look at him. "Hi, yourself, wicked Mr. Calhoun," she said, and to her surprise, he grinned. He had gone on to the bench, but the next Monday at school as she moved between classes, her path was blocked. "Hi, again," he said. "Scared to speak to me at school where one of your brothers will see you?"

"I'm not scared of my brothers. I just don't particularly want to speak to a Calhoun. You've got brothers in school, too."

"What about your parents?"

"My parents will never know. Dad's busy with his work and Mom has a social life."

"I know your dad is a Dallas judge. Does he commute?"

"No, he and Mom live in Dallas during the week. My brothers and I didn't want to leave Verity High so our grandparents are living at the ranch with us."

"So we can't be together in Dallas or out here. Okay, after school, meet me by the Dumpsters. I'll pick you up and we'll go to Lubbock and get ice cream, if you're not scared to risk it."

"Why would I want to go out with a Calhoun?"

"Same reason I want to go out with one particular Milan. Scared?"

"No, I'm not scared of you. What about football practice?"

"I'll tell Coach I've got an appointment in Lubbock. Maybe I will have one if you'll say yes."

She still remembered the thrill over the prospect of going with him. For one moment she thought of all the warnings to stay away from the Calhouns and never trust one. As she looked into his dark brown eyes fringed with thick black lashes, she took a deep breath.

"I'll meet you," she said and from that encounter on, she thought he was the most exciting boy she had ever met. They worked out an arrangement with their two best friends. Her parents thought she was dating Steve Reynolds, someone they had no objection to. Jake's parents thought he was dating Marilee Wilson. He would pick up Marilee, and Steve would pick her up. Then they'd meet and trade places. She would spend the evening with Jake while Marilee and Steve did the same. At the end of the evening, they would meet, trade places and go home.

Their secret dates ended when her brother Tony saw her in Lubbock with Jake. She still recalled how horrified she had been when they fought, leaving Tony with a bloody nose and Jake with a black eye and a bruised cheek. The fight that followed at home with her brother had not been physical, but just as painful, as they didn't speak to each other for weeks. Tony informed the other brothers. Each brother had reacted in a way typical of his personality—Wyatt talked to her seriously in his quiet manner, warning her never to trust a Calhoun because she would get hurt. In hindsight, she should have listened. Nick laid out a grim scenario that she had dismissed as his gloomy dislike of the Calhouns.

She'd disregarded her brothers' warnings. The year she'd dated Jake had been the best one of her life. The man could dance, and they'd had such fun. And he could kiss. With Jake, she had made love for the first time.

While they dated Jake made plans to attend Mississippi State after high school graduation. She could not stop recalling the day they planned to elope. She had dressed in jeans and a T-shirt, the same as every other Saturday in her life, but she'd already had a bag packed. It held a knee-length white silk dress, veil and matching pumps, and a lace nightgown that she could recall with total clarity. Later, after her family had gone, she had deliberately taken them to the patio and burned them in a metal wastebasket, standing by with a hose in case the fire got out of hand. She could still recall standing there and crying. Jake had just disappeared out of her life without a word to her. The next morning she had driven to Rocky Creek, stepped out of the car and thrown her one-carat engagement ring into the creek. She never saw Jake Calhoun again.

Shaking off the painful memories of the past, Madison tried to focus on the chore for the day—the latest painting that she had been commissioned to do for a Dallas oil magnate's office. But she couldn't stop thinking of Jake.

Work on the painting went slowly that week, and she found her thoughts constantly looking ahead to Sunday and their dinner date. Curiosity about why he wanted to talk to her nagged at her. He had to have a good reason. She knew it wasn't a ploy to get with her. And she most definitely didn't want to get with him.

A little before seven on Sunday night she waited in the library of the ranch, which gave a view of the drive to the front. She wore a dark blue dress with a deep V neckline. The dress was straight, clinging to her figure, the narrow skirt ending above her knees. With her hair pinned up on her head, she hoped to look remote, cool, self-possessed. She was still amazed she was going to dinner with Jake. And then she watched him step out of the limo and head for the house. At the sight of Jake, her heartbeat pounded.

She was going out with him again.

Two

The sun was on the horizon when Jake stood at her front door and listened to chimes. He had rarely set foot on this ranch because they would not run the risk when they had been dating in high school. Even when her parents were away, her siblings were around, or the ranch hands, who would have reported back to her dad.

He and Madison had had secret meetings occasionally on the boundaries of their ranches, but those were rare.

He looked at the house as if seeing it for the first time. The Milan family home was different from most ranch homes in the area. The stately Georgian with white Corinthian columns looked like it belonged in the Deep South. Two giant oaks framed the house but outside the fenced, watered yard were smaller, less majestic mesquite trees and cacti. The fine home stood on a working ranch that had prize-winning cattle and probably lucrative oil and gas reserves in the ground.

He stepped up to the door and took a deep breath. An

evening with Madison. He couldn't believe this was actually happening. He still expected her to try to back out, but he knew once they were on their way, she would be committed. Frowning, he pushed the doorbell and listened to the chimes. Had she backed out, standing him up now in a tiny effort to retaliate for their wedding years ago?

Their wedding. The familiar, burning anger started in the pit of his stomach. He didn't want to think about that time in his life or recall anything connected with that day. *Keep this business tonight,* he told himself. Present his case, feed the lady and whisk her back home. He suspected he was going to have to use his best powers of persuasion, but he had an ace in the hole that he hoped would capture her interest and make her agree to his plan. A twinge of guilt rocked him for the secret only he, his parents and his brothers knew. Clamping his jaw closed, he shifted his weight as he reached again for the bell. The door swung open and his breath left him.

Looking sophisticated and breathtakingly beautiful, the woman he faced was stunning. Momentarily, another twinge of guilt stabbed him, but he shoved it aside. Recalling dealing with Pete Milan, the ever-smoldering anger threatened to make him lose his relaxed demeanor. With an effort Jake pushed aside any thoughts about her dad.

"You look beautiful," he said.

"Thank you," she replied quietly, but she didn't look happy about his compliment.

"Shall we go?" he asked.

"This better be good."

"I wouldn't be doing this if I didn't have to," he said softly as she turned away to pick up a jacket. She scowled at him, so he knew she'd heard him. She punched in an alarm code and stepped outside, closing and locking the door behind her.

The driver stepped out of the black limo to hold the door

for her. She climbed into the seat and watched as Jake sat beside her with space between them. He caught another drift of her perfume. It was not a scent he recognized, but it was enticing, filled with the smell of flowers and spice, and a hint of something more.

Jake had been amazed at how much he had thought about Madison all week. He had the detective's information about her, but it had meant little until he was in her presence. He flicked a quick glance over her. She still had the best-looking legs of any woman he knew.

"So where do we get the plane?" she asked as the limo drove away from her house.

"At the Verity airport," he said.

"Your plane or a charter?"

"It's my private jet. We keep company jets in Dallas," he answered as he shifted so he could face her. Her green eyes were on him, steady, veiled, hiding what she felt, but he could imagine her thoughts were as turbulent as his. "Your art career is going well, I've heard."

"I've been happy with it."

"I'm sure you have since that's what you always really wanted," he said, failing to keep a bitter note out of his voice. "I wouldn't think you'd bury yourself out here on the ranch if you have a gallery in Dallas and one in Santa Fe." He kept up conversation but all he wanted to do was look at her. Her green eyes had always captivated him, but now he noticed so much more—her flawless skin, her full lips that he wanted to kiss. He almost groaned as he made an effort to look away. "I'm surprised you like it out here."

"I grew up here. I'm used to it," she remarked, giving him a glance. She seemed more poised, controlled than she had before. "This way I can live in more than one place. I come out here to paint so I won't be disturbed. In town there is something constantly going on or people dropping by. Mom and Dad gave the ranch to me three years ago.

My brothers have their own places. I'm here in the fall until Christmas and I come back in May. The rest of the time I'm in New Mexico or sometimes in a condo in Dallas. Where are you most of the time—here on the ranch?"

"No. I'd prefer the ranch, but I'm based in Dallas, where the home office for the energy company is. I'm seldom here because of taking care of business. By the time I'm forty, I hope to retire and be a full-time rancher because that's what I love."

She nodded and became silent, looking out the limo windows. The airport was on the east side of Verity and they drove through the wide main street that had once been a dusty cattle trail before the town sprang up. They left the shops and stores, passing the oldest homes in the town, two blocks of wooden Victorian-style homes, some single story, some two or three stories tall, still occupied and taken care of with flowers and the oldest trees in Verity in the yards. Then they reached a tall Victorian house in a block by itself, the last before leaving Verity. She looked at the familiar sight, a wooden three-story surrounded by a three-foot wrought-iron fence and a front gate hanging on one hinge. Windows had been broken out. Weeds and high grass filled the yard, while the two tall oaks by the house were overgrown with vines. Without thinking she glanced at Jake.

"There's the Wrenville house. Remember when you and Wyatt and two other football players went out at night to search through the house?" Madison asked.

"Like everyone else, we didn't find anything and got chased out by the sheriff. I don't think anyone today has much interest in the place."

"You and I have ancestors that were killed there—both in love with Lavita Wrenville according to the legend. Her father drew his weapon and all three men were shot and killed, but it was never clear who shot the other," she said.

"Before she died, Lavita said that one of them lived long enough to tell her who shot who. According to legend, she wrote it down and hid it before she died. I wonder if we'll find anything when 2015 occurs."

"Your brother will know before anyone else. By 2015, there may not be many who care. According to the legend, the city can do what it wants with the house and property in 2015. I heard that's why your brother is sheriff. So many people wanted him to run because he's so honest and everyone trusts Wyatt. He'll be sheriff when they can finally tear down the house and look for the letter," Jake stated.

"I think the reason they wanted an honest man is more because of the part of the legend that says Lavita died a very wealthy woman and her money is hidden somewhere in the house," Madison remarked. "If Wyatt finds anything, he'll turn it over to the city and make public which man shot the others.

"I'd like to hear what happened. Did the Milan shoot the other two? Did the Calhoun? Or did her father shoot both of the men who wanted to marry his daughter?" she said.

"Or," Jake said, "they all could have fired their weapons at the same time and then fired again. It never was made public how many times each man was shot."

"I'm surprised the townspeople didn't insist," Madison said.

"The Milans and the Calhouns were even more influential and powerful in those days than now," Jake said. "If they didn't want the killings made public, they wouldn't have been. And Lavita could have been the one who kept it all secret. We'll know someday. Twenty-fifteen approaches."

She shivered. "I don't know why you and Wyatt decided you wanted to search for an old letter about killings in another century or even for a mythical fortune."

"We were kids," he said. He smiled. "Your brother

doesn't scare easily. We were just curious and we both wanted new, fancy cars."

She became silent again, not mentioning that she had been scared for both Jake and Wyatt that night. Looking at the house now, she wouldn't want to hunt for an old letter or even a fortune in there.

"Jake, we'll have a quick flight to Dallas. Why not talk about what you want on the plane? There's no possible interruption there."

"That sounds agreeable. The weather's good and it should be a smooth flight." The sun had reached the horizon when the plane lifted off the runway, but once they were airborne and headed east there was more light as they chased the sinking sun.

"Might as well enjoy happy hour while we fly. What would you like to drink? We stock a full bar."

"Any chance of conjuring up a raspberry tea?" she asked.

He told the flight attendant what they wanted to drink and shortly, the man reappeared with a tall, chilled glass, which he offered to Madison, and a beer for Jake. When they were again alone, she sipped her drink and smiled. "You have the formula—this is delicious."

"Glad you like it."

Madison leaned back in her chair. "Let's cut to the chase, Jake. There's no need for polite chitchat—why do you want my land? For what possible reason would you expect me to invite you onto the ranch?"

Her eyes were wide, green and thickly lashed, and he was mesmerized. A streak of sunlight streamed through the window, bathing her cheek in golden light, highlighting her fully rosy mouth. He inhaled deeply and then realized she was waiting for him to answer her question.

"This goes back generations before Lavita Wrenville.

This was the earliest Milans and Calhouns. You know there's a legend of hidden treasure on your ranch."

"That old tale went around the family before I was born," she scoffed, sitting back and shaking her head. "All of us looked for it. I've heard men from a couple of past generations were supposed to have searched endlessly. No one has found anything and most of us came to the conclusion long ago that it was merely a myth."

"Still, it persists though all the generations."

"Just try to get a kid to stop looking. Tony and his friends have probably dug up a total of a dozen acres with all their hunting for gold. Look at you and Wyatt, hunting for Lavita Wrenville's fortune, which might not ever have existed."

"I can imagine. I've hunted with my brothers on my side of the boundary that divides our adjacent family ranches. Since part of the boundary line is the river, the boundary keeps changing slightly. Going back to my great-great-grandfather Henry Calhoun, there was a sketchy map. No one in our family ever had interest in sharing it with anyone in your family. I'm guessing that maybe in the early days one or more family members offered to make a deal and split, but your family member refused."

She smiled and his heart turned over. Desire heightened and he suddenly wanted to see her laugh, to hold her, dance with her—to have the past vanish. That wasn't going to happen.

"So you have a map." She shook her head. "I didn't think there was a shred of truth to the legend."

"Occasionally, legends are built on something—maybe not always exactly the way it's stated in the legend, but something caused the legend to spring up."

"It's hard to believe there is a treasure hidden on our ranch."

"That's not so far-fetched. There was a lot of lawlessness in the early days, train robberies, later bank robberies. People just hiding something. This is a vague, damn poor map and has never made any sense to anyone in my family. I don't think it will to you, either, but you know your land better than any outsider."

"All these years. Why would your family even have a map?"

His gaze ran over her features, her skin that looked soft, flawless. He wished she had worn her hair down.

"No one can answer that one. The map may be bogus, although it has been in the family for generations. I'd bet that someone or maybe several in my family have tried to sneak onto Milan land to find the treasure."

"I'm sure you're right there. Why wouldn't they? These ranches are big with wide, open land. Someone could easily search without anyone knowing about it." She sipped her tea and shook her head. "So there's really a map. All these years, actually all my life, I've heard the legend and heard various relatives talk about searching for it, but by the time I was grown, I just figured it was a tall Texas tale with nothing to it." She sat back, smiling at him. "So you want permission to come on our land to search for the treasure."

"That's not all." As her big green eyes focused so intently on him, he forgot the map, the treasure and his whole purpose for the evening. He wanted to close the last bit of distance between them, place his hand behind her head, wind his fingers in her hair and pull her closer to kiss her.

"There's more?" she asked, looking at him with curiosity in her expression.

Desire raged in him, blatant and hot, until he remembered their past and then anger returned, smothering his feelings for her. He inhaled deeply, looked away and focused on his purpose.

She leaned closer. "So what else is there, Jake? What

else besides a map have you kept secret all of these years and never told me when we were so close?"

"At the time we were in high school, we talked about it. It was mysterious and exciting to speculate about the legend, even though neither one of us believed it. Of all the people in both families, you and I seemed the most willing to forget the feud."

"Yes, and I know we both thought the idea of a hidden treasure was exciting. I'm surprised you didn't tell me about the map then."

"I didn't know it then. There's a rule in our family—no one gets told about the map, and sworn to keep it in the family, until he or she is twenty-one years old."

She laughed, a soft sound that played havoc with his insides again and made him forget what he was after.

"That's probably why your family has kept it secret all these years. Kids talk."

"Probably," he said, smiling at her. "When you heard the legend, did the version you heard mention a shoot-out?"

"Yes. I heard there were Milans and Calhouns who would discover each other searching for the treasure and the Milans would run the Calhouns off our land."

"Did you ever hear if any were killed?"

"Yes, but truthfully, I was a kid and didn't pay that much attention to talk about someone who had lived generations ahead of me and who I never knew."

He sipped his beer before he continued. "According to the Calhoun version of the legend, wherever the treasure is buried, your ancestors and my ancestors had a gun battle. Two Calhouns were killed and three Milans. They're buried in shallow graves where they had the gunfight. This goes back to the first generation of each family to settle here and it was before both families had their own cemeteries. Now we have our own burial ground and I imagine you do, too."

"Yes, we do."

"I want the bones of the Calhouns brought home. Hopefully, we'll find the treasure, which is yours since it is on your land."

"You want bones," she said, frowning slightly. "You could search every day for the next ten years and never find graves or bones or treasure, if it even ever existed. I can't imagine that's what's behind this dinner," she said, beginning to sound angry.

"Just one more thing besides the bones. There's supposed to be a deed one of our ancestors was carrying. It was a deed won in a poker game. According to the story my family tells, the deed gives the Calhouns rights to a large part of the McCracken place to the east of us all along the border of his ranch."

"A deed to the McCracken land," she said, staring at him while she seemed lost in thought. "If that exists, it's worth more than any treasure you could possibly dig up."

"Jeb McCracken is mean and ornery and has fought with every neighbor," Jake replied.

"That includes my family. There are people in town he's aggravated. He's left unpaid accounts all over this county and he's spent more than a few nights in jail for brawls on the weekend in town. No one would regret seeing you get a chunk of that property." She stared at him with a speculative curiosity in her eyes. "My ancestors are supposed to have been in that gunfight, also. Suppose we find the deed with my ancestors. Are you still going to claim it?"

He gave her a faint smile. "Not if their name is on the deed or it's in a bony skeleton hand."

She had to smile then and he felt another punch to his insides. Her smiles and her laughter had always been his undoing. He ached to reach out and touch her.

"I have no intention of searching long. I want you to look at the map I have and see if you can recognize anything. You probably have aerial photos of your land, all sorts of photos. If anything seems likely, then I'd like a chance to see if the deed exists, see if a treasure is buried with them and get my ancestors' bones to take back for a proper burial. I have time in my life for that now and it would please my grandfather."

She laughed softly, shaking her head. "You don't seem the type for this. Why do I feel as if I better look at this from all angles, that you're up to something—like surveying my land to drill for oil or gas?"

"All I want is what belongs to the Calhouns—namely my ancestors' bones and the deed to the McCracken land if that exists. I'm not going to do any surveying, I promise you."

"According to the old legend, the treasure is what caused the feud in the first place. Your great-great-great-grandfather and my great-great-great-grandfather came out here after the Civil War. What I've always heard is they found gold in a deserted house in Tennessee during the war. Later, my relative stole away your relative's fiancée right before the wedding and that's when the feud started. Then they fought over the gold and the woman they both loved, but a Milan killed a Calhoun, so the Calhouns rode in at night a week later and burned down a house, killed a Milan and carried off the woman in question, adding to the anger between the two families. The fight has continued until present day. I guess we have a truce of sorts now."

"That matches what I've always heard about the beginning of the feud," he said. "That and when they fought, there were several Milans and several Calhoun brothers, plus an uncle."

She shifted, recrossed her legs, distracting him totally. She sat quietly, so he remained quiet, letting her think about what he had said. She turned to the window and his gaze traveled slowly over her. She was twisted slightly in her seat, the neckline of the blue dress gaping a fraction, revealing the full rise of her breasts, her skin pale and creamy. The temperature in the plane jumped and he wiped his brow as images of long ago tormented him. Her waist was as tiny as ever. How well he could remember the feel of her in his hands. He had to stop thinking about the past, had to avoid erotic memories that set his heart racing.

Jake remembered her dad and that last night before he was going to elope with her, and the tantalizing memories vanished, replaced by anger, dulled by the passage of years, but still there.

She turned back while he was still looking at her neckline. She shifted slightly. "Jake, I have to think about this. We'll be in Dallas before long, so we might as well go to dinner. I'll consider your request and by this time tomorrow, I'll give you an answer."

"That's great, Madison," he said, feeling a stab of satisfaction. He was certain she wanted to discuss his proposal with her brothers. He hoped not her father.

Their pilot announced they were approaching Dallas and as they lost altitude, the sun was low on the horizon. By the time they were in the limo on the way to the restaurant, darkness had set in.

In a short time they were seated in a darkened corner table in a small private room. Lights were low, music from the piano player in another room was muted.

"So you got a private room for us. I didn't know there was any such thing for just two people. I'm impressed."

"That's one reason I like this place. There are only three of these rooms." He paused when their waiter arrived to take drink orders.

"Little chance of interruptions here by people who know either of us," she said as soon as they were alone again.

"That's right. You can barely see your hand before your face, much less who else is in the restaurant. Do you still like fried chicken better than anything else?" he asked, looking at a menu. He glanced up at her.

"No, like so many other things, my tastes have changed. I see lobster on the menu—that's what I'll have."

"Excellent choice. I'll have the steak," he said, watching her while she had her head bent slightly over her menu. The candle flickering in the center of the table highlighted her shiny brown hair and rosy cheeks. Again, he wished she had worn her hair down the way he liked it best. He should forget what he liked best about her and leave anything personal a closed subject.

In minutes the waiter returned. He uncorked a bottle of white wine, gave it to Jake to taste and then poured two glasses after Jake's approval.

As soon as they were alone, Jake raised his glass. "Here's to finding the treasure."

With a faint smile, she touched his glass with hers and heard the faint clink of crystal before she sipped. "That's a safe, innocuous toast," she said.

He smiled in turn. "I thought so."

"I'm still thinking about your request."

"If I'm successful, you'll get your treasure, I will find a deed and get the bones of my ancestors for a proper burial. We both win."

She tilted her head to study him, sipping her wine while she sat staring. "Why do I feel there is more to your request than you're telling me? I find it a little difficult to trust you. You better not have manufactured this map yourself."

He held on to his temper. "My dad took the map to someone in Chicago who could tell him the approximate age. It dates back to the mid-nineteenth century. That's good enough for me. I'll give you a copy of the letter and you can contact the people in Chicago yourself."

"I'd like to see the original map. Will it disintegrate if it is handled?"

"Not if it's handled carefully and you don't intend to pass it all around. But you don't get it until we have a deal."

"You don't trust me," she said, bitterness filling her voice and anger flashing in her eyes, for an instant igniting his own fury, which he banked immediately.

"Should I?" he asked, trying to curb his feelings and get back to amicable dealings with her.

"Of course. You did at one time," she reminded him sharply. Looking away, she took deep breaths. Spots of red were high on her cheeks. She sipped her wine and gradually her breathing went back to normal before she faced him again.

He'd give her time to think it all over; he just hoped the flare of animosity hadn't killed the deal. Again, he had a flash of guilt for what he had kept from her. But then he thought about her father and stopped worrying about the secret he harbored.

Madison ate in silence while she mulled over his proposition, studying it from every angle because she didn't trust him. She suspected he wanted badly to drill on her land and she wondered how much of wanting his ancestors' remains was because he wanted to lease part of her ranch. Why hadn't this come up years earlier or with some other Calhoun? And a deed and map? She had never heard of either one. Were they both hoaxes so he could get on her ranch? She wondered what was behind Jake's request. She couldn't keep from feeling that it was something to do with wanting to drill on their property.

What did she have to lose? That's what she couldn't figure. So he saw her land up close—she was certain he'd seen aerial photos because they were in the county records and on the internet. If he found the treasure, he had said she could have it. He simply wanted his relatives' remains and the deed if there was one. While part of any ranch around here, including the McCracken place, would be a real asset, he would have to fight McCracken to get it.

She couldn't believe a deed and his ancestors' remains could be all there was to his request.

She glanced at him to find him watching her. His thickly lashed midnight eyes were seductive, mesmerizing. And guileless. He looked honest, trustworthy, open—all good qualities, yet she couldn't believe the proposition was simply what he was telling her and nothing more.

Caught in his steady gaze, she forgot the legend, the treasure and the proposition. Instead she remembered Jake's eyes filled with passion, a silent emphasis to what he did with his hands and his body. She had loved him deeply.

Instantly she broke off that train of thought and tried to think about her schedule tomorrow, his proposition, anything to escape memories that twisted a knife in her heart.

No matter how she turned his request in her mind, she couldn't think how there could be an underlying motive and anything else for him to gain without her knowledge if she said okay to him.

"If I say okay to your proposal," she asked him, "what are you going to do? Go out there with your shovel and start digging around?"

"Of course not," he replied, smiling, his smile giving her heart a squeeze. He was so incredibly handsome and appealing and a smile made him doubly so. "I'll get a crew from my ranch hands—not too many—about five. I want you to study the map and see if you can narrow down the location. There is no earthly way I can. You know your land, and if you don't, one of your brothers should."

"I'm no geologist. Suppose I can't tell anything?"

"Then you and I will work on it together, but I'll bet you'll look at the map and come up with some possibilities for the area."

She thought about what he was telling her as she put

down her fork, her appetite suddenly gone. She wondered what she could do to make sure she didn't get cheated.

"You didn't eat much," he observed a few moments later.

"It was delicious, but I don't eat much most of the time and I've been busy thinking about your proposition."

"Take all the time you need. You don't have to give me an answer tomorrow night for that matter. I can wait. Want to go dance?"

"No, thanks," she replied, smiling at him. "This is sort of a business dinner and I have no interest in dancing. Too much on my mind. I'd step on you," she added, broadening her smile.

"I wouldn't mind, but we can sit out the dancing." He leaned forward, reaching across the table to take her hand. The instant her fingers touched his warm ones, she couldn't get her breath. The air around her heated and her body tingled. That slight contact sizzled from her head to her toes and then settled low in the center of her being, a hot torment that made her ache to be in his arms and brought back memories of Jake holding her close, kissing her passionately, making torrid love to her that drove her wild.

"Truce?" he asked and she barely heard what he said as she stared at him. Something flickered in the depths of his eyes and for one brief instant, his fingers tightened around hers and his thumb ran over the back of her hand.

"You always did have the smoothest skin ever," he whispered, his voice husky, a thick whisper, while his eyes blazed with such hot desire that she felt as if she would melt. At the same time, she wanted him to pull her toward him, to take her on his lap while he wrapped his arms around her and kissed her senseless. Closing her eyes momentarily, she tried to stop thinking about the past with him, the love she had thought they had shared. Love that he had smashed the way someone would break a crystal goblet by throwing it down.

She yanked her hand free and looked away, gasping for breath and hating that she had lost control so obviously that he could not avoid knowing exactly what she was feeling and thinking. He could see how much he could still affect her and she hated it.

"I guess we have a truce," he said. His voice was raspy and she realized she still had an effect on him, too, giving her both satisfaction and annoyance.

"Truce for now," she replied without looking at him.

"When you're finished, we can head home. You can think about what I've offered."

She nodded. "Then I'm ready to go back," she said, wondering if they would say goodbye at her door and if she turned him down, if they wouldn't see each other again. She didn't care and she wasn't too interested in accepting his proposition, except there were possibilities that would be good for her family.

She continued to think about all he had told her while he paid the bill and they returned to the airport. They barely talked, which seemed so odd in some ways. Long ago, she could talk to him endlessly and never tire of it.

Finally, as they flew back to Verity, she turned to him. "I think I would like to have our ancestors' remains have a proper burial, also. If you remember, I've always been interested in our family tree and our history. The treasure—that seems a tall tale to me, but who really knows? It's a generous offer to turn the treasure over to me if we find one."

"Somehow, I think we might be more likely to find bones than treasure. If we do find treasure, that's a good payment for your agreement to this," he said. His long legs were stretched out in front of him, his booted feet near her. When they had boarded the plane, he had shed his jacket and tie and unbuttoned his collar. He looked relaxed and he still appeared open and straightforward, but she couldn't shake the feeling that in some way, he was slipping something past her.

After another lapse of silence between them, she sat up straighter and turned slightly to face him. He sat watching her.

"If we do this and do find bones, how will we know whose bones are Milans and whose are Calhouns?"

"Take them to the county medical examiner. We can get some kind of DNA test and they can sort out the two families."

She nodded. "That sounds reasonable. And I walk away with the treasure?"

"Absolutely."

She lapsed into more silence before she broached the topic. "I know you want to lease some of my land for your energy company. Why not go elsewhere? It's a big world."

"So it is, but your land looks promising and is an area that we think may be a big play. It's also cheaper and easier for us because it's close to our headquarters. Labor is available here. Trained men who do this if we need to hire more. It's dollars in the bank instead of going off a long distance."

"That sounds reasonable. Suppose we put a high, high price on this."

"You can price yourself out of the market, but energy companies, I think, are generous when they want something. Are you going to give us a chance?" he asked, looking at her and smiling, making her heart turn over again. Longing swamped her again. Too easily he could trigger those feelings.

"Don't push me, Jake," she said and he became silent again.

She thought about his original offer, still trying to look at it from all possible angles. When they stopped in front of her house, the driver came around to hold the limo door. Jake accompanied her to her door.

"Want to come in a few minutes? Would your driver mind?"

"No, he'll wait. He's getting paid for whatever he does."

She unlocked the house and turned off the alarm. "We'll go into the study," she said, glancing at Jake to see him looking around.

"I forgot—you've never been inside this house. Seems ridiculous in some ways, but understandable in others. My ancestors would be turning over in their graves if they knew I'd invited a Calhoun inside."

Jake smiled again. "I still feel the feud is arcane, ridiculous. Come into the present."

"I agree, but we decided long ago to stop fighting it," she said. As he walked beside her, he looked around. "Is any of this art hanging on the walls yours?"

"Not in the hallway, but in here it is," she said, leading him into a study that held a large wet bar. "The painting over the mantel is mine," she said and he crossed the room to look at the large painting of a field of bluebonnets, a tall oak in one side of the field and a stream running through it. "You're not a contemporary artist. This is a beautiful painting and you're very good."

"Thank you. The painting on that wall by the window is mine, too," she said and he crossed the room to look at the painting of three horses in a field, a cowboy holding the reins and standing by one. "That's good, Madison. Very impressive. I can see why you've been a success."

"Thanks. Would you like a drink?"

He shook his head. "No, thank you. Let's just talk."

She motioned with her hand. "Have a seat," she said, sitting and crossing her legs, pulling her skirt to her knees and catching him watching her.

"I've been thinking about this all evening, Jake," she

said slowly, watching him intently. "I will in fact give you a final word tomorrow night...." She wouldn't commit until she talked to her brothers; after all, she had to protect Milan interests. "But I'm thinking about accepting your proposal." She speared his eyes with her own. "Under one condition."

Three

Jake tried to avoid showing any emotion, but his heart-beat sped up and he had a flash of satisfaction. She was going to agree to let him on her ranch. He barely paid attention when she said she had a condition. He couldn't imagine anything she could come up with that would stop him from accepting.

"Sure. Let's hear it," he said.

"I want to take a couple of my ranch hands and accompany you."

As if cold water had been poured over him, his enthusiasm chilled. "You don't trust me? Madison, if I surveyed your land, it wouldn't get me any further with you on signing a lease," he stated, sitting up straight in the chair. "I don't intend to survey, but why would you want to go with me?"

"First of all how would I know if you found the treasure if I wasn't along, except pure trust that you would inform me about it? That isn't going to happen," she said, her voice sounding cold and harsh, something he had never heard from her before.

"I expected you'd want one person to go with us—I figured one of the men who works for you. There's no reason for you to go with us and it would be a waste of your time to have to sit and watch us dig."

"You said nothing about someone who works for me going with you."

"That's your decision."

She faced him, looking calm and composed again, the flash of anger gone. She shook her head. "That's my condition. Take it or leave it. I go or you don't."

He stared at her a moment and then shrugged. "Sure, come along. If you think it over tonight and still want the same agreement, that's fine. You have yourself a deal," he said, holding out his hand. "If we find the treasure, you get it. I get my ancestors' remains. We'll just have to see if we do find a deed, what it says and who the land goes to. You go with me to search for the treasure."

She placed her hand in his to shake while she smiled at him. "Deal."

Her hand was warm, soft, and when they looked into each other's eyes, he realized it might be torment to work with her beside him every day. He released her hand and the moment was gone, but it had dampened some of his enthusiasm. He didn't want to get emotionally involved with her again and he didn't like this constant flashback to that time in his life when she meant everything to him.

"I can go in tomorrow and clear my calendar. I don't think we'll search for more than a week, but I'll clear my schedule for two weeks just in case. I can be ready to go Tuesday. What about you?" he asked.

"My time is my own. I think it would help if you would give me a copy of the map and let me study it. We need to have an idea where to go before we start. If you can send me an electronic copy of the map tonight when you get home, I can start studying it. Then tomorrow night, if you'd like, you can come over and look at maps of the ranch with me. You're a geologist—I'm sure you can figure out some things from those photos of the ranch."

"Sure. That'll be good. I've already scanned in the old map, so I can send it easily."

"Good. We'll get started tonight."

"You're going to lose a lot of time to work on your art."

She shook her head. "No, I won't. I'll take my sketch pad with me—because I don't intend to dig. You're the one so eager to do this."

"You're the one who will benefit from it if we're successful," he reminded her. "But you don't need to dig so much as one shovelful of dirt."

He stood. "I'll go home and send you a copy of the map. Give me about an hour."

At the door he paused. "Thanks, Madison, for agreeing to let me do this. Hopefully, it will be a productive venture."

"I hope so. Thanks for dinner," she said, following him into the hall.

"I'll call you when I get home," he said, walking away, aware she stood on her porch and watched him. As the limo pulled away, she still stood on the porch—a small figure in the moonlight.

They were going to search for the treasure together. Not what he had expected, but it was okay. The main thing was she had agreed to let him look. He hoped he succeeded in finding everything he was searching for. Again, guilt assailed him, but all he had to do was think about the day he had planned to elope with her. As he rode, he pulled out his phone to call his brother Josh, but there was no answer.

He didn't want to call Mike this late because Mike had a two-year-old son and he would be in bed.

He called Lindsay next to tell her. His sister was jubilant over his success with Madison.

After finishing his call with Lindsay, he thought about Madison. Was she looking forward to the search? He knew she hadn't accepted because she wanted to be with him. It had been obvious that tonight had been a strain on her and she disliked being with him.

He didn't understand the anger he had glimpsed in her eyes a few times. Why was she angry? She had done what she had wanted to do and put her career first. He shrugged, refusing to worry about it. It no longer mattered. He was honest enough with himself to admit it still hurt sometimes but he had put it in perspective and moved on.

As they reached the back door of his ranch house and his chauffeur stopped the limo, Jake opened the door. "Thanks, Chauncy," he said, tipping his chauffeur in spite of the generous salary he paid.

"Night, Jake," Chauncy said, following his boss's orders for informality when it was only the two of them. Chauncy drove on to the garage to park the limo and go to his spacious apartment over the six-car garage while Jake entered his house.

In a short time he called Madison to tell her he had sent the map copy. Their conversation was brief and then she was gone.

Then he spread the maps on a table in his study and compared the ancient one with the one he had of Madison's ranch, which was an aerial view. He had already picked out what he thought the most likely places to search, but he wanted to see what she chose. He could hardly believe it. He'd wanted to do this for a long time and now it was finally going to happen. Adrenaline pumping, he could barely contain his excitement. He had energy to burn, so turning off the light in the study, he went to the gym to work out. If all went well, he was in for some hard physical labor in the coming week.

Monday morning Jake flew to Dallas and went to his downtown office on the twentieth floor of Calhoun Energy. His office was half the floor with a reception room, his private office with its own entrance, the executive conference room, a room with a bar, a bathroom and a small workout room. On the floor above were two penthouse apartments with terraces.

Before Jake could call, Josh phoned and said he was on his way up. Jake was glad Josh was in town. Even though he had an investment in Calhoun Energy, he had his own hotel business and was gone more than he was in Dallas. In minutes his brother came striding into his office. His straight dark brown hair was neatly combed and he looked every inch the successful hotel mogul with his gold cuff links catching the light as he swung his arms. The gray suit and matching tie provided contrast for his brown eyes and dark looks.

"Good morning. How did it go last night?" he asked, sitting in a leather chair facing Jake, who leaned back in his chair behind his desk. Morning sun slanted through the floor-to-ceiling windows behind him.

"Excellent. I have permission to search on her ranch."

"Hot damn! That's perfect. So she bought it. Any stipulations?"

"Yes, she had one. The hitch you predicted," he said, thinking each sibling reacted in a customary way and Josh was the cynical, study-all-angles-first brother.

"She wants someone from her ranch to go along," Josh surmised.

"She does. More than one. In fact, she's going with me."

"Uh-oh," Josh said, narrowing his eyes. "Do you think she wants to renew old times?"

"Not even remotely. She doesn't trust me and she wants to see for herself."

"She's going to join you if you dig for buried treasure?" Josh asked, making a tent of his fingers in front of his chest. One booted foot rested on his knee.

"No, she won't dig. I'm guessing that she'll watch or sketch while she waits. Whatever she plans to do, she is definitely going with me."

"Don't ever trust her."

"I don't think you need to give me that advice," Jake answered.

"I suppose not. So what happens if you find something and she's there?"

"The treasure is hers as we planned. We get the remains. If any remains are Milans, she can have them."

"What about the deed? If it's there, she'll see it."

Jake nodded. "If it's buried with the treasure, yeah. If we find it, she's going to want to see it. At that point, I'll drop the part about the McCracken land because she'll know that I knew all along if there was a deed to land, it was Milan land."

Jake sat forward in his chair. "You know, I wonder if it's a tall tale—that our ancestor won part of the Milan ranch in a poker game and the deed was buried with that treasure."

"You'll have to take on about the bones of our ancestors like they mean the world to you."

"I'll worry about Madison. If that deed exists, I want it. According to what we were told, the deed would give us Milan land all along our border and that would be fabulous."

"I think so," Josh said, his brown eyes twinkling. "You'd

get revenge for old man Milan telling you that you couldn't marry Madison, to never go near her again."

"I don't care about revenge. That's the past. If we have a deed to part of their ranch, I want that Milan land. We're not the only company going after leases there," Jake said, knowing that all his siblings owned shares in Calhoun Energy, just as he had an investment in Josh's company.

Josh ran his fingers through his hair that sprang away and curled in a tangle. "Have you called everyone to tell them?"

"Yeah, I called you, too, and no one answered."

Josh grinned. "I got your text. When you called, I was with…a friend."

"The redhead?"

"No, she's gone. Sandy is a brunette. You'll meet her, maybe. Or maybe not."

He paused as they heard voices outside the office and he watched their oldest brother, Mike, and their sister, Lindsay, appear from his private entrance.

"Good morning," Mike said, standing and gazing at his brothers with wide dark brown eyes. Locks of his curly black hair fell slightly on his forehead. He shed his brown leather jacket, draped it on a coatrack by the door and hung his brown broad-brimmed hat on the rack.

"Come in and sit. Where's Scotty?" Jake asked about Mike's two-year-old.

"Home with Mrs. Lewis."

"Lindsay, I didn't expect to see you this morning."

"I had to get some supplies and Mike talked me into coming. This is great news."

"Madison was suspicious of my motives at first, but then she bought it and said that I can look for the treasure," Jake explained and all three siblings cheered. "You two have a chair," Jake said and Mike sat in the other leather chair while Lindsay took a wingback.

"And Madison thinks the deed gives you land from the McCracken place?" Mike asked.

"Right," Jake replied. "From what I've always understood, until now, no one outside our family knows about the deed."

"Thank heavens," Josh remarked.

"Madison's going with me on the dig. That's the only way she would agree."

"That's bad news," Lindsay remarked, frowning. "You can bet her brothers will be thinking up ways for her to take advantage of this. She'll try something sneaky."

Mike shook his head and rolled his eyes. "She wants to get back together with you."

"No, she doesn't," Jake answered. "Madison doesn't trust me to tell her if I find the treasure. It's that simple."

"Watch her. I don't think it will be that simple," Mike said. "I agree with Lindsay. Don't ever trust a Milan," he said and Jake's eyebrows arched.

"What happens if you do find the deed?" Lindsay asked.

"I show it to her and claim the land."

"You can just act surprised there really is a deed," Mike said. "She can't blame you for feeling uncertain about it."

"I won't need to act," Jake remarked dryly. "I will be as surprised as hell if we find a deed or anything else. I don't really think that legend is true."

"Something got it started and it makes sense. You know our ancestors shot and killed Milans and Milans shot and killed some of our ancestors, which is part of what started the feud," Josh said.

"A woman got it started. She planned to marry a Calhoun and ran off with a Milan," Mike reminded them.

"You know Madison doesn't trust you," Josh remarked.

"I don't really care," Jake replied. "If there is a deed and that deed will stand up in a court of law, then part of the Milan ranch is ours. Maybe the best part of the Milan ranch." All were silent a moment and Jake figured the others were thinking about the prospect of owning part of the Milan ranch just as he was.

"What a deal," Josh stated, his brown eyes on Jake. "This may get the old feud fired up again."

"I hope we're all more civilized today than to go shooting at each other," Jake said. "We may start searching tomorrow. I'm going to her house tonight to look at aerial photos of her ranch and hear her theories on where to look. I sent her a copy of the map last night."

They speculated on where the digging would take place, as they had all studied the map and the aerial photos of the Milan ranch.

"All we can do is wait and see," Mike said. "Call one of us each night and give us a report and we'll call the other two."

Jake agreed.

"That old legend," Lindsay remarked. "It would be funny if it turned out to be true."

"It sounds likely to me," Mike added, glancing at the others.

"I go back and forth about it," Jake said. "I first heard it from Grandad. He said a Calhoun had a box of gold and he was trying to get away from robbers—"

"It might have been just the reverse," Mike said. "The Calhoun ancestor may have been the robber trying to escape a posse.

"They've also said the shoot-out was over a Calhoun's fiancée who ran off with a Milan and they had the shoot-out over her," Mike stated.

"That's what Grandad always said. He said the Calhoun got her back because he killed the Milan," Jake said. "The deed was won by a Calhoun from a Milan and was supposed to say clearly that the land belonged to the Calhouns, and the deed was with a box of gold coins."

"The ranch boundaries we have now weren't clear back in the time that shoot-out happened, but that started the feud," Mike said. "Myth or truth? Maybe we'll finally find out with our generation.

"I'd like to come with you," Mike added, "but I think it would cause trouble with Madison Milan to have two Calhouns."

"No," Jake replied. "She won't want the Calhoun brothers going along, or our sister."

"Frankly, I don't want to go," Lindsay said.

Josh stood up. "I've got to go. I leave for L.A. in a few hours. Good luck, bro," he said, looking intently at Jake. "Sorry, but I don't think you'll find anything. If a treasure is on that ranch, it's a needle in a haystack."

"I'll text all of you each night."

"Good," Mike said, standing with the others. "Good luck to you."

Jake gave him a thumbs-up. He watched as his siblings left and then he sat, turning his chair to look out over Dallas while he thought about the old legend and the Milan ranch. Was it really true or was this a wild-good chase? If there was a buried treasure, was there any hope of them finding it? Actually, it might be buried on Calhoun land because to all his family's calculations it was close to their boundary. Through the years there had been plenty of searching on the Calhoun side, but to no avail.

He thought again of Madison, remembering her perfume, the way the blue dress had clung to a figure that still took his breath away. She was a beautiful woman, poised and confident now. He hadn't slept well last night with her filling his dreams. Memories of making love to her had plagued him, waking him, leaving him hot, sweaty and wanting her, something he didn't want to feel. They had been kids when they had thought they were in love.

What had been a significant difference at nineteen and

sixteen no longer mattered at thirty-two and twenty-nine. When he looked back on it now, he had to admit that they had been too young to marry, but at the time it hadn't seemed that way.

Because of Pete Milan's heavy-handed manner, Jake had never thought about the man being right until the past few years. All he could remember was her father warning him to get out of Madison's life and disclosing that she had already accepted his offer to open art galleries for her and get her showings in the best exhibitions in the Southwest and along the West Coast—if she would call off the wedding. Her father's promise had probably saved her several years of struggles and had made her a legitimate working artist. Evidently that was what she'd wanted the most. More than him. Jake had known instinctively that his own dad would have agreed with Pete Milan and said they were too young to marry; his mother never liked any of the Milans anyway.

He thought again of Madison, remembering holding her soft hand last night when they had the handshake on their agreement. Could he work with her and keep his hands to himself and resist flirting with her? Did he really want to resist? Was she still off-limits to his heart? Wisdom answered yes. She obviously didn't feel kindly toward him or want to recall the past. What would it be like to be with her every day for the next week or two?

Madison bent over the map and aerial photo spread before her as she made notes. For several hours she'd tried to focus her thoughts, but too often she realized she was staring into space, lost in thought about Jake and their time together last night. She had been shocked at how handsome he looked—far more than when he had been nineteen years old. Worse, he was even more appealing to her as a man than he had been as a teenager.

She had never known if her parents had any inkling of the depth of her feelings for Jake Calhoun. It didn't matter now.

One time their foreman, Charley, had come around the garages and seen her in her car at midnight. He had asked if her parents knew she was out and he had told her to go back inside. She had gone back, climbing in through her open bedroom window and sitting there, watching in the dark until she saw Charley disappear into the bunkhouse. She had climbed out again and taken a truck, driving across the ranch in the moonlight to meet Jake. That had been one of the last times they had been together before the night they had planned to run away and get married.

For days she had wondered if Charley had ratted her out to her dad, but when nothing happened, she decided he had not. Charley had always kept an eye on them for her dad, especially the boys, and she never liked Charley because of it, although now that she was grown, she understood why he had. She'd never even told Jake about the incident because it hadn't seemed that important.

How in love she had been with Jake! She had thought he was the most wonderful person she had ever known. She remembered his dark brown eyes last night and her racing pulse when she had caught him looking at her lips while desire blazed in his eyes. What was it going to be like to work with him every day for the rest of the week? Could she hold up her end of this expedition?

She thought about crossing the porch with him last night when they had come home after dinner. If he had taken her into his arms to kiss her, would she have stopped him? Breathless, she thought about Jake's kisses. Would she have been able to stop him?

Tonight he would be in her house to look at her photos and maps. Could she eat with him tonight, work with him and still resist him?

This morning she had called the man in Chicago who had validated the map. He had searched his records, finally calling her back and telling her the map was authentic. The thought of seeing the actual map that was a tie to her past was exciting.

She had sent a text to all her brothers about the search. Tony had called immediately after he received the text, which was typical because he could be impulsive. Nick's call had come later in the afternoon after he had thought things over. Wyatt had needed the most time to think it all over, as he tended to view everything more objectively than any other family member.

Tony had started arguing instantly. "I don't think you should go. I should. You can't trust Jake Calhoun, or any Calhoun about anything. You should know that. I'll call him."

"No, you won't," she'd said patiently. "Just wait. I'm taking two men with me and we'll watch all the time to see what is going on."

"Don't do it. The Calhouns are up to something."

She had argued with Tony for half an hour before she finally got him to promise to stay out of it until she asked for his help.

Wyatt and Nick had been easier, but the message had been the same—they didn't trust a Calhoun. She had promised them both she would be careful and she'd keep all her brothers informed of what was happening. She had promptly put them and their warnings out of her mind. She could take care of herself and her ranch.

She looked down at the map again, even though she had it memorized by now.

Would the map really help them? She thought of all the warnings and pushed aside her worries. Men who had worked for them for years would be with her, so there was nothing to worry about.

Except maybe falling in love with Jake Calhoun all over again.

The thought came unbidden. No, she assured herself, she would not fall in love with him again. Still, a nagging doubt tormented her. Jake still set her pulse racing and the slightest contact with him was electrifying. For the next few days she would be with him from sunrise to sundown.

Why hadn't he married? Was he wondering the same about her? Regardless, she intended to guard her heart. She suspected he wouldn't want to fall in love again any more than she did.

She forced herself to get back to her notes. Promptly at six, when she had told him to appear, the doorbell rang. She opened the door and looked into Jake's dark brown eyes before his gaze drifted slowly to her toes and back up again, taking in her jeans and plaid shirt, and making her tingle all over.

"You look gorgeous," he said in a husky voice.

She was thinking the same about him. He wore a navy Western shirt, boots and tight jeans. He had a wide-brimmed tan Stetson on his head, creased in the familiar local style. He held a brown leather briefcase.

"Thank you. Come in," she said, stepping back. "Let's get something to drink and then go look at the map and pictures I have. I have a casserole in the oven and we can eat whenever we want."

"Show me the way," he said. "I wonder how long it will take me to get accustomed to entering this house and not feeling as if I'm committing a crime."

She smiled. "You shouldn't feel that way now."

"This was the forbidden palace. Any of your family around tonight?"

"No. They're in Dallas. They're rarely out here except at Christmas when we all get together. Even our Christmas celebration has been in Dallas the last few years. I'm sure you see my brothers some because they're around. Nick has a home in Dallas, Wyatt has a home here in Verity and Tony lives on his ranch. We all have our own ranches now, but only Tony lives on his year-round."

"Sure, the illustrious sheriff of Verity, Wyatt Milan. I see Tony sometimes in Verity or at rodeos. Your brother Nick is probably too busy trying to become president someday."

She laughed. "He would like to be, but right now, he's too busy being a state representative."

They stopped in the kitchen to get drinks. As he helped, she caught him watching her. His gaze made her heart beat faster and she wondered again how she would get through the next few days, or weeks, working with him.

"Let's go to the library," she said and when he walked beside her, she was aware of him, close, almost touching her.

"Madison, I'm sorry about your sister-in-law."

Madison nodded. "Thanks. That car wreck was a tragedy. In public Nick does fine, but he's had a hard time dealing with the loss. He was so excited because she was expecting."

"That must have been rough."

"You've had your own losses. I'm sorry about Mike losing his wife to cancer. At least he has his son."

"That helps, and keeps him busy. It's been hard for him trying to be both mom and dad for Scotty."

"That's tough and so sad."

"Mike's happy with his nanny and Mom comes to stay sometimes for a month at a time, so that's helped him. The baby is a cute little fella and that cheers him up. He tries to stay upbeat because of Scotty."

"Do your brothers know what you're doing?"

"Oh, yeah. I don't think they really expect much to

come from it. This isn't the first search for that fabled buried treasure."

"I know. It'll probably be another wild-goose chase, but the map is fascinating. I'm anxious to see the actual map. It gives a little more validity to the legend, but finding something buried anywhere on this ranch is kind of mind-boggling."

Carrying her tea while he carried a beer, she led the way to the library, a large room filled with floor-to-ceiling shelves of books and pictures.

She stopped at a long table filled with maps and photos. "Those are aerial photos, but over here are satellite pictures," she said, waving her hand and moving to a computer and an iPad toward one end of the table. "You can see these photos better and move around or expand them. Look at whatever you want."

"This is impressive," he said as he bent over one of the aerial pictures. "I haven't seen this one."

"No, it's not out there for the public. That's one of our pictures. Look at the map and then look at the aerial photo and the satellite maps of the ranch. Maybe you can find some landmarks in them that are similar." She glanced up and saw him staring at the open neckline of her shirt. Self-conscious, she wanted to reach up and button one more button, but she didn't want to draw that much attention to herself. His eyes met hers and she was ensnared in his dark gaze, desire filling her as she stared at him. Realizing what was happening, she looked away. To cover the flush that heated her cheeks she pointed to the aerial photo.

"Look at this, Jake."

He shifted his attention to the papers on the table and while he studied them, she looked at his profile. He was clean-shaven, his thick black hair combed neatly. Jake's lashes had a slight curl over seductive dark eyes that could hide his feelings easily. The past few moments had shaken her. Desire had overwhelmed her, and he had felt it, too. She hoped that didn't happen again during the coming week. She had to go with him. No way would she trust him even if she had her men go with him.

As she studied him, she knew the week or weeks ahead would be a strain. It would help if he hadn't gotten more appealing through the years. He was breathtakingly handsome. Did other women see him that way, or was it just an effect he had on her?

Jake sat in front of the wide-screen computer to look at a satellite map.

She stepped closer to sit near him so she could look with him. As she did, their shoulders brushed lightly, the slightest touch, but she was acutely aware of the contact. She forced her mind back to the screen.

"These maps should help in our search," he told her. "I've studied the old map off and on through the years. In my judgment, it looks as if the location is along the banks of Rocky Creek." He picked up his briefcase to set it on his knees to open it. "I brought the original. I got it out of the vault."

"That's exciting, Jake," she said in anticipation.

He removed a box with a glass front. Inside was the yellowed, torn and wrinkled map. He opened the box and lifted it slowly, gently, his well-shaped hands holding it gingerly.

"Maybe you should leave it in there and we'll just look through the glass," she said, though she wanted desperately to hold it herself.

"No. We can see it better this way."

"Jake, can I touch it? It's a connection to my first Texas ancestors."

"Hold out your hands," he ordered. When she did, he carefully placed it into her open hands, his warm fingers brushing hers. The contact of their hands made her forget the map for a few seconds as she looked up at Jake. He sat so close, and as she looked into his dark eyes she felt a flash of longing.

"Thank you," she said, the words coming out in a whisper. She remembered the fragile map and looked at it, drawing a deep breath. "Jake, this feels like a tangible tie with the past."

"I hope it's a damn tangible tie to a real buried treasure."

She examined the map, thinking about the ancestor who had carried it. "This is fantastic. It makes me wonder about those early-day Milans. If there is a treasure, was it ill-gotten gains, or gold that had been acquired legitimately?"

"We'll never know the answer to that one."

"Here. You can have it back."

"Just place it close here where I can compare it with the satellite map that shows everything the most clearly." Jake studied the computer and she looked at a picture that showed her ranch, all the trees, bushes, the house and other buildings and roads. He adjusted the map on the computer and pointed to a place with his finger. "I want to compare this stretch along Rocky Creek. There are some trees on the map, but trees die or are cut down. New trees crop up beside them. I don't think we can go by the trees on the map."

"Probably not," she said, placing the antique map gingerly near the computer. He moved so close his arm brushed hers. He reached into his briefcase to retrieve a flashlight. "Can you hold this?"

She took the flashlight and he turned back to shift the map, moving it slowly and carefully. The additional light showed the map more clearly.

"Now look—these circles—it's printed here, I think, 'rocs.' Look at this aerial picture along the creek bank."

"There are rocks, but there are about a dozen more places along the banks where there are rocks on both sides."

"Yes, but look. The creek curves here in the picture," he said, pointing. "The creek curves here on the map. It looks like the same place," he said, leaning closer to the table.

"That's true, but then look here." She pointed farther up on the screen. "Here's where I thought it looked most like the electronic copy of the map you sent me. There are rocks, the creek curves just slightly around a sandbar, but in all these years the creek could have swallowed up the sandbar. You see what I mean?" She looked around to catch him studying her so intently she forgot the map momentarily. He drew a deep breath and turned back to the map.

"That's a possibility." He let out a heavy breath. "I never expected this to be easy. People have been hunting for that treasure all my life and probably since the late nineteenth century."

"Maybe you should sit and study these maps while I get dinner on the table. After all, this is the first time you've seen these photos of the Double M Ranch."

"Sure you don't want kitchen help?"

"I'm sure," she said, leaving Jake looking at the computer screen, pausing at the door to look back at him. Light shone on him, giving midnight glints to his black hair. Was she going to be able to work with him without rekindling feelings she didn't want? Some feelings had already ignited. And that's what scared her.

While she got drinks and dinner on the table, her thoughts stayed on Jake.

When she returned to call him for dinner he shook his head as he stood. "I've found four likely places so far. We'll both look after dinner. I have the feeling the longer we look, the more places we'll find," he said, walking beside her to the kitchen.

"That does smell good," he said and she smiled.

"A simple dinner—baked tilapia on angel-hair pasta

with artichoke hearts and sun-dried tomatoes. I have a sauce for the fish or lemons."

They entered the kitchen, which had glass-fronted cabinets built in the late 1900s when the original part of the house was constructed.

"Nice kitchen," he said, looking around.

"All the equipment is about three years old, which was the last remodeling. It is a nice kitchen. I've grown up in it and I love it, high ceilings and all."

He held her chair and she was acutely conscious of every brush of his hands, every look he gave her. What did she still feel for Jake? She didn't want to answer her own question. A week ago, she would have told herself that she had no feelings for him, but after being around him, responding to him in startling ways, she had to admit that she was still attracted to him.

"We have some fancy homemade garlic bread."

"Did you do all this?" he asked and she shook her head.

"I'd like to say yes, but I didn't. Jessie Lou cooks for me now and Harriet cooks for the men. Dad deeded this ranch to me. He and Mom don't care to stay here at all any longer. I inherited the staff, too, so Ethel still cleans three days a week and her daughter comes once a week to help. Ethel and Jessie Lou still live here on the ranch and Ethel's husband still works, too."

"I don't know about the cleaning, but you have the best cook possible."

"I think so. Jessie Lou isn't here tonight, but she was here until five. She and Harriet are still both wonderful cooks. Some things don't change."

"I remember some great picnics we had where you brought something Jessie Lou made."

She smiled. "Remember her chocolate cake that got ants all over it? You said you weren't giving your slice up to a bunch of ants and juggled the cake around to let some of the ants run off and then ate it, ants and all."

She laughed while he grinned and shrugged. "And you were so afraid I had ants in my mouth that you wouldn't let me kiss you that afternoon or that night."

As she laughed, his grin widened and her heart turned over. Desire flared to life, a hot torment that made her want him badly. She should never have opened the door on memories of fun times with him. She looked down at her plate. Her appetite had fled and she tried to think about something besides Jake.

"We had fun," he said quietly and there was silence that stretched between them. She didn't want to look up and meet his probing dark eyes because he always saw too much of her. He could hide his feelings better than she could.

"I guess we should each pick the places we want to look and list them," he said briskly to her a few moments later. They were back in the present and she tamped down the memories that threatened her heart.

He sipped his iced tea. "Did you get over your fear of snakes?"

"No, I did not. I still won't swim in Rocky Creek."

"How are you going to go traipsing around out there? You know we have an abundant snake population."

"You said you're bringing some men. I'll have two, plus you and me. We ought to make enough noise to scare the rattlers away. And if we don't, I also figured that one of you will have a pistol."

"One of us will. I keep one in the pickup."

"There," she said, smiling at him. "You can kill a snake if we encounter one."

Through dinner they discussed the search and when they had finished, they sat sipping more tea, talking about the treasure. "We better look at the maps," Jake said. "I'll help you with the dishes."

"No need. I'll just put the leftovers in the fridge and rinse our dishes for the dishwasher. You go back and keep looking."

"I'll do the cleaning and you go look," he countered. "You've never had this chance with the actual old map and it is clearer than the copy. I insist," he said, taking dishes from her and blocking her path.

"So I see you are as stubborn as you used to be," she said.

He smiled. "Just as stubborn as you. Some things don't change."

She realized they were getting back where she didn't want to go. Her smile vanished as she returned to the table to push in her chair. "Let me put up the leftovers," she said, picking up the pasta bowl. He took it from her, his hands closing over hers. Startled, she looked up at him and drew a deep breath.

"It's all yours," she said and left quickly. Desire ignited each time they made contact. Sometimes when they were close she caught him looking at her with a gaze that clearly conveyed he wanted her.

She hurried out of the kitchen, feeling him watching her walk away. How would she get through being together with him every day for the next week or two? This wasn't working out the way she had imagined.

Four

She pored over the maps swiftly and stuck by the list she already had. She wanted to finish and get him out of the house.

When he joined her, she showed him her list, pointing out each place and waiting while he looked. Jake got a legal pad from his briefcase, turning to look at her while he held both of their lists.

"We have three places that are the same, so those will go to the top of the list. Your first choice is my second, so we'll put yours first because you know your ranch better than I do."

She marked the three locations on each map. "Look at our other choices so we can decide and get them listed."

She pulled her chair close to his, far more aware of him beside her than the map in front of her. "I think my number four should be next."

It took another hour to get everything listed and finally

he stood and put away the original old map in its glass box and then into his briefcase.

"Jake, I hope we find something," she said, walking him to the door. "I don't care about the money so much, but if the treasure exists, it's a tie to the past. I'm sure it's true that there was a gunfight and both families had members killed. We do need to give those bones a burial place." She stepped out onto the porch with him. The September night was cool, the black sky dotted with twinkling stars. "Thanks again for letting me see the original map. I'm fascinated by it."

"You're a romantic," he said in a deep voice. He stood only inches from her and his dark eyes were shadowed. She had an urge to step into his arms and raise her face for a kiss, but she fought it and moved back.

"Can you be here about six in the morning? We can get started early and get out on the ranch by the time the sun rises."

"Sure. We'll be here. Want me to get lunch packed?"

"No, Jessie will do it each day. See you in the morning."

"Thanks for dinner, Madison."

"You're welcome," she said, thinking how polite they were being with each other. Better that than the flashes of scalding longing to be in his arms and make love again. She stepped back and watched him walk away. As soon as he drove out of sight, she went in and closed up, setting the alarm on the grounds around the house.

The next morning she was on the driveway with her two men and a nearby pickup packed with gear and food. The outside lights were on because it was still dark, without even a hint of the dawn to come.

It had taken her an hour to dress this morning. She had tried to avoid thinking about Jake, but whatever she selected, she thought about wearing for him. She finally decided on a long-sleeved blue Western shirt, jeans, boots and a brown wide-brimmed hat. Her hair was in a thick braid down her back. A tingle of excitement made her edgy. She couldn't wait to get going and start the search. It wasn't about the gold. Honestly, if he had said he wanted half, she would have agreed instantly. It was about the tie to the past and the Milans who had lived generations ago. It would mean the legend was a true accounting of events of the past, which she hoped it was.

She spotted headlights coming up the ranch road. When they drove into the light she saw two pickups. Jake drove his big black pickup with someone seated beside him and two in the backseat. Another red pickup followed with two men.

Jake stopped and climbed out, slamming the door and striding toward her. His black Western hat sat squarely on his head and his tight jeans emphasized his small waist and long legs. He wore a navy-and-red-plaid Western shirt and looked filled with energy because of the spring in his step.

"Good morning."

"Morning, Jake," she replied. "This is Darren Hopkinson and Stoney Rassmussen. Darren and Stoney, meet Jake Calhoun."

The men shook hands. "We're ready," she said.

"It's your ranch, so you lead the way and we'll follow," Jake suggested.

"Sure. Let's go," she replied and they parted to get into their trucks.

She turned down a dirt path that ran past houses, outbuildings, the ranch office, corrals, barns, sheds. Finally they left the graveled road and took a dirt road in the opposite direction, bumping over rocks and dips in the road, running over weeds that grew in the center between the ruts.

She knew where she was going and could have driven it with her eyes closed. She had learned to drive on these ranch roads. She glanced in the rearview mirror and saw Jake's black pickup behind her, the third pickup coming last. From the list they had selected, they had mapped out a plan to start on the north side of the creek and search eastward. They both agreed that the map looked as if the treasure had been buried along Rocky Creek.

By dawn, they had reached the trees and in a short time approached the only bridge over Rocky Creek on the Double M Ranch. Trees lining the creek bank blocked the sunlight so the vehicles still had on headlights. Madison reached the creek first.

"Miss Milan," Stoney said beside her. "Wait. Look at the bridge."

She stopped the truck, her headlights illuminating the far end of the bridge. One of the tall cottonwoods lining the creek had fallen on the end of the bridge, preventing any vehicle from crossing.

"Nobody's said anything about a tree falling on the bridge," she said, turning to look at Darren and Stoney, who both shook their heads. Switching off the motor, she stepped out while Stoney and Darren followed her. Jake stepped out of his truck.

"We can get that tree moved out of the way. It'll just slow us down, but it's not going to stop us," Jake said. "All the men come with me and we'll move it."

"We'll cut it up later and get it out of here," she said, looking around. "What could have caused that tree to fall? It looks healthy and there hasn't been a storm recently. That tree hasn't been down long," she said more to herself than anyone else.

She waited in the truck and in minutes the men all returned. Stoney and Darren climbed into the truck while Jake stopped beside it. "Someone cut that tree down so it would fall on the bridge. There's someone who doesn't want us hunting for this legendary treasure."

Startled, she stared into his dark eyes. "That's foolishness. That was a temporary setback and it won't stop any of us. Who would do that anyway?"

"Not my family," he answered. "We have too much to gain. Just be careful. That may merely be a warning."

She shivered and looked at the tree that had been pulled away from the bridge.

"We'll go ahead as we planned," she said.

"Why don't you let me drive around you and cross the bridge first? No one will drown if the bridge collapses, but it won't be fun to go into the creek in one of these trucks. Let me see if anyone tampered with the bridge."

"Very well, but I'm not scared to go first."

"I'll go." He left and climbed back into his truck. He drove around her and she followed, letting him get completely across before she followed.

Within ten minutes he switched off the engine and parked. She pulled up beside him and the last pickup stopped. Men climbed out while Jake joined her.

"This is our first stop. Now you call the shots. What do you think? Look here or start walking?" she said.

He studied his map. Bits of sunlight slipped between leaves and branches, highlighting his raven hair. "Gather round," he said to the others.

The day was warming and because of rains farther north, the narrow stream gurgled and splashed over rocks nearby.

"Before we start, I want to talk to all of you," Jake said. He pushed his hat to the back of his head and the broad Western brim framed his face.

"Myth or truth, we're going to try to find the legendary treasure. If we find any gold or even just bones that are remains from a gunfight, everyone will get a bonus of five thousand dollars—Milan hands and Calhoun hands alike—from me."

Jake paused as the men grinned and applauded.

"You'll have earned it. This will be tedious work. If we find nothing, you'll get a thousand dollars above your regular salary just for volunteering for this."

Again the cheers and applause caused Jake to wait. "Okay. Madison and I have been over the maps and this is the area we picked to start. We're just going to spread out and start digging along Rocky Creek this morning. Good luck and let's dig."

Jake was a take-charge person—she had known that back in high school when she'd watched him on the football field as quarterback. They had both been in the math club and he had been president, taking control of the meetings and being decisive when problems arose. She had been vice president and she could remember some clashes they'd had, too.

Jake turned to her. "You might as well do what you want—look on or sit it out, but if you sit, watch out for snakes."

"Sure, Jake," she said, pulling out her map. She began to move up the creek, but after a few feet saw a likely spot. She sat on a rock and studied her surroundings, the mesquite, cactus, small plants and, at the water's edge, grasses and weeds.

Jake walked up and sat beside her. "What do you think?"

"Now, I'm not so sure."

"It's a start. You can stay right here."

"I'm getting my sketch pad." She stood to follow him but slipped on loose rocks. Instantly his strong hands closed around her waist and held her. She grasped his arms to steady herself and then looked up into his brown eyes, her breath shortening as his gaze lowered to her mouth and her lips parted.

She stood there, immobile, aware of his hands on her,

of hers holding him, and of how close they stood. Would he kiss her? Her eyes widened before she stepped away quickly. "Thanks for keeping me from going into the creek," she whispered, not knowing what else to say to him.

He nodded, but didn't respond.

Shaken more by Jake's hands on her than by almost falling, she moved away, walking a few yards upstream before she stopped. He stood watching her.

Maybe coming along hadn't been a good idea, after all, she thought. Yet she knew she was the only one who could deter Jake if he wanted to do something that none of the people with Milan interests thought he should.

Moments ago her body had blazed with desire. She had wanted his kiss. That's what had shocked her the most. Over eight or nine years ago, she had thought she was completely over him, no longer feeling a vestige of attraction or love for him. She had thought she'd put him away with childhood memories, boxed up and stored as a keepsake of a long-ago phase of her life. She'd thought she'd blocked him out of her mind. Well, she had been wrong. Obviously. In one moment with his hands locked around her waist, she had wanted to wrap her arms around his neck, step close and kiss him.

She couldn't trust Jake. She would never trust him. Right now, he could be up to something. He could have offered to let her have the treasure so she couldn't see that he had any hidden agenda or ulterior motive.

It would take a long while and lots of time together for him to win back her trust. If he ever could.

She got out her pad and sketched for about two hours, but then laid aside her pencils.

Feeling a need to stretch her legs, she started moving away the rocks that would have to be relocated before anyone could dig in this area. She hadn't moved more than half a dozen rocks when Jake's hand closed on her wrist.

Startled, she straightened to face him. "What?"

"Stop. You don't need to be doing heavy labor."

She laughed and pushed tendrils of hair from her face. "I'm all right. I'm not fragile."

"You'll be surprised what will hurt in the morning if you keep that up. Leave this stuff to us. You can break out the lunch shortly back at the trucks or we can drive up here."

"This land is too rough for that."

"No, it's not. That's what our trucks are built to do. Come on, we'll go get two of the trucks." He took her arm to steady her over the rugged terrain and she went with him, again aware of his fingers on her arm. This time he seemed oblivious of the contact, which helped a degree.

At the trucks he opened her door. "This time let me lead. You follow me."

Jake held the door for her and she climbed in and he took the lead pickup. When they reached the place where three men were digging, they parked.

"Go back to your digging," she said. "I'll get lunch ready."

She washed her hands from a jug of water she had brought for that purpose. Opening the back of both pick-ups, she spread out Jessie Lou's sandwiches, chips, and opened the coolers filled with ice, pop and water. She set out two homemade apple pies and a container of whipped cream, then rang a small bell to call everyone.

Jake and the men grabbed the camp stools he had brought or sat on nearby logs or rocks. Jake came to sit beside her on a slab of sandstone.

"So far, it's a bust. The only progress is that we can eliminate this area."

"You said that you didn't expect this to be easy," she

stated. "We're just getting started. Over the generations my family has scoured this part of the ranch for the treasure, although I don't think they went along the creek a whole lot because creeks move as years pass, which means, in some spots, the treasure could possibly be in the bottom of the creek."

They ate and went back to work. She cleaned and put away leftovers, finally finishing and pulling on her gloves to move some more small rocks again. She picked up one and a thin snake slithered away, trying to get beneath the adjoining rock. She cried out with fright and yanked it up by the back end, swinging it and throwing it toward the creek as fast and as hard as she could.

She heard laughter and turned to see Jake not far away. "I believe you've gotten over your snake fears."

"No, I haven't," she snapped, "and stop laughing. That wasn't funny." She shivered. "I couldn't do anything else to get it away from me. I can't kill one."

"If you'd waited a second, I would have killed it," he said, grinning. "Good toss, by the way. Looked like a copperhead, though. I should tell you they don't usually travel alone."

She shivered again. "I'm taking a break," she said, turning her back on him to walk to the truck and climb inside. She glanced back to see him still grinning, making her even angrier. She hated and feared snakes as much as ever. When she had grabbed it up, she hadn't stopped to think. She just wanted it away from her. She had to admit she was ready to call this quits and leave her ancestors' bones where they had been buried in the 1800s. She was too aware of Jake. Being close to him was beginning to awaken feelings she hadn't had for years, feelings she thought she was over and didn't want to have again. She was hot and tired already from moving rocks. She thought back to the pre-morning hours. Had the tree blocking the bridge been a warning? She couldn't imagine who would do such a thing or why. Her brothers didn't want her doing this, but they wouldn't stoop to cutting down a tree to achieve what was only a temporary delay.

She wanted to be back at the house painting and enjoying her quiet life. From the moment Jake had appeared in the hardware store, he had done nothing but stir up trouble for her.

Later in the afternoon Jake dug in the shade of a cottonwood at the edge of the creek. He had shed his shirt and the muscles in his back rippled as he worked. He was muscular, strong, and she could recall the feel of his bare back as she'd run her hands over him, kissing him. He had been a tall, lean, bony teen then. Now he had filled out, become a man.

The temperature had risen and she was hot, but the heat of the day wasn't her problem. It was the memory of being locked in his arms, naked, her body held tightly against his. She could recall his hands moving over her, caressing her. She didn't want to remember, but the sight of him shirtless triggered the memories with a clarity that surprised her. "Jake," she whispered and then clamped her mouth shut.

She didn't want to get to the point where she longed to have the past repeat itself. If every day of this search would be like this, she would have to quit because this was bringing torment into her peaceful life.

She shifted to watch him dig. He was forming a large, shallow hole. He stopped and glanced around as he wiped his brow, and when he saw her watching him, he leaned on the shovel and simply stood there openly staring at her. She wondered what he was thinking.

He didn't say anything, and after a few moments he went back to work.

They worked until dusk and then they all climbed into

the pickups to drive back to their ranches. At her house, Jake stopped to talk to her. She thanked the men with her and then stepped out of her pickup to wait while Jake parked and climbed out.

"Jake, you still have a long drive to get home. Why don't you tell the men to bring clothes tomorrow and bunk down here and you can stay up here at the house? We have room."

"If you're sure, I'll take you up on it and I think they will, too. If anyone doesn't, he can drive his own truck. Are you going again tomorrow?" he asked.

"Of course," she replied even though she had been on the verge of canceling for the past four hours.

"I'll see you in the morning, then," he said, standing with his hands on his hips, staring at her. She wondered what was going through his thoughts because he looked on the verge of saying more to her. Instead, he got in his truck and drove off.

She wanted to shower and to change clothes before she ate the dinner Jessie Lou had ready for her to reheat. As Madison emerged from the shower, her phone rang and she answered to hear her father's voice.

At first they talked briefly about nothing in particular and then he said, "I hear you allowed Jake Calhoun to dig on our property today."

Startled that he knew, she realized one of the ranch hands must have informed him. All of them knew about Jake because she had asked for two volunteers to go with her. "Yes, I did. I told all my brothers. Jake has a map that seems authentic."

"Aren't you running some risks by letting a Calhoun traipse all over our ranch?"

"It's a calculated risk, I guess. But if we find the treasure I get it."

"So what does he get?"

"His ancestors' remains." She heard her father's derisive grumble and she continued, "Plus there may be a deed giving them McCracken land from a poker game."

There was a moment of silence. "Be careful, Madison. You can't trust him one inch. I think you're foolish to allow this, and if I were you, I'd call the deal off tomorrow. The treasure won't be worth whatever he's up to. You can believe that he is up to something more than wanting his ancestors' remains and an old deed that might not ever stand up in court."

"I'll be careful," she said patiently, wishing he hadn't found out and hoping he didn't hear about the felled tree on the bridge. "I have Darren and Stoney with me. We'll be careful and they've been warned to watch him and his three men."

"You think about what I've said—you should just run him off."

"He's shared his map with me because I said he could do this. It will be brief, probably three or four days."

"Be very careful. You should know you can't trust him in any way."

"I'll be careful. Don't worry."

"That goes with being a dad," he said. "Think about what I've said and tell him you've changed your mind. No good can come of this."

"All right."

"Take care of yourself."

"I will. Thanks, Dad," she said far more cheerfully than she felt. As they said goodbye, she stared into space, seeing Jake's dark eyes and remembering moments during the day. Was there a reason to be suspicious? Was he truthful or deceitful? Had she been taken in again? And which person had reported to her father? Someone left behind, or Darren or Stoney?

In all of this, just who could she trust?

* * *

As Jake returned from dropping the men off at the bunkhouse, he saw a familiar pickup heading toward his back door. He got out of the truck and waited while his younger sister pulled up beside him and got out.

"Hi. Did I come at a bad time?" she asked.

"Never," he said, smiling at her. Six years older than Lindsay, he felt like a second dad to her. He watched her walk through the gate—the only blonde Calhoun as well as the only blue-eyed Calhoun, but she had the Calhoun bone structure, their height and their deep love of ranching.

Her sandy-blond hair was in a thick braid that hung over her shoulder.

"I had an errand anyway, so I swung by. I thought you'd be back and I wanted to see how the search went today."

"Come in and we'll have a beer while I give you the details. But I can tell you right now, we didn't find any treasure, bones or deed."

"You're just getting started."

"Thank you for being kind enough to keep from telling me I'm on a hunt that is hopeless."

She grinned. "I'm glad you're doing it. It would be fabulous if you found the deed. That would be sweet revenge and serve the Milans right for all the things they've done."

"Let it go, Lindsay."

"I can't let it go with Tony Milan. If I ever catch him on my ranch I've got buckshot and I intend to let him have it."

"Lindsay, listen to me. Don't do it. I don't want to bail you out of jail over something stupid like that. Take him to court—follow legal channels against trespassing. Don't go off half-cocked and do something you'll regret."

"Then he needs to stay off my ranch."

Jake caught her shoulders and turned her to face him. "I mean it. Don't get yourself in trouble over a Milan."

"Sometimes, Jake, you are such a wet blanket," she said, wriggling out of his grasp.

"Yeah, well, dealing with me is still a whole lot better than standing up in front of Judge Milan."

"Judge Milan is in Dallas and he would have to recuse himself. Don't get your coattails in a twist. I won't go after Tony with buckshot, but he can be really annoying, and at the last horse auction, he was there and outbid me for a horse I wanted and— Don't you smile. When he trespasses, I can't call the sheriff because the sheriff is his brother. Sheriff Milan is not going to do one thing to harm his brother."

"No, he probably won't. Why is Tony trespassing?"

She sighed. "He has when one of his animals gets into my pasture. We had a fence go down and his stock overgrazed that section before I found out—"

"He has to get his livestock back, Lindsay. You don't have a case. Cut him some slack. I just want you to be protected. Don't give the sheriff an excuse to cause you trouble."

"I hope you find that deed and it gives you acres and acres of Milan land."

"You're too bitter, Lindsay. You're the youngest Calhoun, but you sound like Granddad."

"Tony Milan is like a pesky fly you can't swat. Enough about them. Tell me about today." Her long legs kept pace with him as they went to Jake's back door and entered the house.

"I have to shower, Lindsay," he said as they walked down the hall to the kitchen. "I'm filthy and hot."

"Sure. Go shower. I'll get the beers."

He left, hurrying to shower quickly and dress. He didn't want to keep her waiting and he was ready to sit and relax.

He found her on the patio. With the setting of the sun the weather had cooled. He had enough lights to illuminate his patio and enough of the kinds of plants and lights to repel bugs.

He sat half facing her. "I'm ready for that beer."

"You talked Madison into letting you search for Calhoun ancestors' bones. How was it today when you had to go with her?"

"It was fine. We can both keep the old anger and ill feelings in check. We've had a lot of years to get accustomed to the idea and to practice."

"You haven't been around her during that time. You haven't even spoken to her since that night her dad threatened you."

"No, I haven't, not until this past week. We didn't find anything today, but we're just getting started and I'm hopeful there's a thread of truth to the old legend."

"It could be true in every way and a big treasure could be buried on their ranch, but finding it may be impossible after all these years. Especially if it is buried around Rocky Creek the way you think it might be. Creeks change course over the years, unfortunately."

"I'm hopeful, and with her men and mine, we've got a large enough crew to cover a good-size area."

"Well, I'll keep hoping." She sipped her beer and gazed at his pool.

"How's the ranch?" he asked, always slightly amazed by his baby sister buying a sizable ranch and then running it herself. She had a fine foreman, but Lindsay did a man's work daily on the ranch. All of them had a strong love of ranching, particularly Mike and Lindsay, who lived all the time on their ranches.

"Everything is fine."

"Good deal. I'll put steaks on the grill if you'll stay."

"Sure. Let me help," she said, getting up to walk to the kitchen with him.

They talked about ranching all through dinner and as

soon as she put the last dish in the dishwasher she turned to him.

"I'd better go now. I know you've probably got emails and texts and things to answer since you've been away from the office so long. You'll be up and going early tomorrow, I guess."

He nodded. "Be glad to have you stay."

"Thanks but I've got to go."

He walked beside her to her car.

"Good luck with this, Jake. I sure hope you find that deed."

"I do, too. I'd like to face Pete Milan with it. I'll have to settle for handing it over to his daughter, but the judge will hear about it. If we find it," he added.

She slid behind the wheel and he closed her door.

"Thanks for coming by. It's always good to see you, Lindsay."

"Send me a text if you find anything."

"I will. All of you will get one. I dug as much and as fast as I could today and I will again every day. This is our chance to hunt for that deed."

"Night, Jake. Thanks for the steak."

He stepped back from the pickup and watched her drive out of sight, the red taillights disappearing around a curve, before he turned to go into the house.

He wanted to look once more at the maps and aerial photos. He hoped they weren't missing the right location. He longed to get the deed and get some Milan land. It would be payback, but also, it might be a dandy place to drill.

He thought about Madison. Part of him hadn't ever gotten over her. He still couldn't view her the way he did other women he had dated and then told goodbye.

This opportunity had come when he didn't have a woman in his life. Maybe that heightened the impact of seeing her. In spite of all his hurt and anger over the years, she still made his heart pound and he had to battle desire.

She still felt something, too. It was obvious. She wasn't happy that she did. That was also obvious. Anger simmered in her constantly, little flares of it showing, although he thought they both were doing a commendable job of being civil to each other.

He wanted her, wanted to kiss her, to seduce her. In spite of his fury, his body still responded to her.

Could he seduce her and then walk away? Perhaps the anger would enable him to do that. Time would tell.

Her room was still cloaked in predawn darkness when her cell phone rang. Madison reached for the phone and groaned. She ached all over.

"Good morning." Jake's voice was cheerful, filled with eagerness and energy, and she wanted to hang up on him. "Are you going today?"

"Yes," she mumbled and heard him chuckle.

"A little sore?"

"Yes, I am." She made an effort to try to stay awake.

"I hate to say, 'I told you so.' I can give you a rubdown if you want me to come early this morning."

"No," she said, coming more awake. "How can you be so cheerful?"

He laughed softly. "I'll see you in a little while."

She switched off her phone and sat up, groaning and rubbing her shoulder. "Ugh." She could imagine Jake arriving looking fresh and energetic and eager to go. With a whimper she stepped out of bed. The smell of coffee was faint and she guessed Jessie Lou already had breakfast ready. Moving carefully, Madison headed to her closet to get her clothes for the day.

When she entered the kitchen, more tempting smells

filled the house. "Good morning," she told Jessie Lou, who turned and pushed glasses up her nose with her wrist.

"Morning. This is an early start."

"Everything smells good."

"Help yourself. I'll cut and toast some of my bread and get you an egg right away. There's orange juice."

"I told Jake he and his men could stay here tonight. He accepted the offer and he'll be here for dinner."

"I'll be glad to see him."

"Can't say the same for my family. Dad already called to tell me I'm making a mistake," Madison said as she poured a glass of orange juice.

"Your dad dislikes the Calhouns in a giant way and he doesn't trust any of them."

"He feels strongly about the Calhouns, that's for sure."

"The judge had a run-in with them when he was young. He and Jake's dad both bid on all that land that Lindsay Calhoun has now. Mr. Calhoun won. The judge has never forgiven him."

"That's too bad Dad didn't get the land because it adjoins Tony's ranch. I don't even remember."

"You were away in college."

Madison tilted her head. "You know what happened. Do you think I shouldn't have let him on the ranch?"

"It's not for me to say. I haven't seen Mister Jake in a long time. I'll tell you after I see him. I suppose I will see him since you asked him to stay here. I always liked him until he up and hurt you," Jessie Lou said, staring up at Madison through wire-rim bifocals.

"That's in the past," Madison replied. "What about the lunches? Can I help you with them?"

"Everything is packed in the picnic basket or the big cooler. You have another cooler for water and a cooler of bottled drinks," she said, turning off the stove and spooning the scrambled eggs onto a plate, which she handed to Madison.

"Thanks, Jessie Lou," Madison said, getting her toast and sitting to eat breakfast. Jessie Lou had already placed a bowl of sliced strawberries, kiwi and blueberries on the table. Madison glanced at the clock, wanting to be ready when Jake arrived.

She ate quickly and got showered and dressed. An hour later she watched him emerge from his truck.

To her annoyance he looked just the way she had expected. Sexy and handsome in his Western shirt, tight jeans and Stetson. His stride was long and brisk.

"Good morning," he said. "You don't look as if you suffered any from yesterday."

"I'm great," she said, smiling at him while hoping she really looked that way. "Ready to go?"

"Absolutely," he replied. "You lead the way again."

"Sure. According to our plans, we'll move along the same side of Rocky Creek today."

"See you there."

She watched him walk away, her gaze running across his broad shoulders, down to his narrow waist and long legs. Even with all the cowboys, he stood out because he was the tallest and the best-looking and had a manner about him that conveyed his confidence. She realized how long she'd stood watching him and climbed into her truck where Darren and Stoney waited.

The day was a repeat of the previous one except for the slight differences of lunch and she didn't encounter a snake.

Jake dropped the men at the Milan bunkhouse and then drove to her house. She stood waiting at the back gate, holding it open.

He picked up a satchel he had brought and locked his

pickup. He waved the bag. "I assume the invitation still stands?"

"Of course. Jessie Lou is cooking and I think she stayed this late just to say hello to you."

"Can't wait. She is one fine cook," he said, closing the gate behind them. "You need your latch fixed," he said, jiggling the gate.

"I know. I'll show you where you can put your things and where you'll be staying. Come on." His wavy hair was tangled and he hung his hat on the rack in her back entryway as he came in.

Enticing smells of baking bread and a pot roast mingled in the air. They entered the kitchen and Jessie Lou set a covered bowl on the counter, turning to smile at Jake.

"Mister Jake, I think you've grown even taller."

Jake gave her a big smile. "Jessie Lou, it's good to see the best cook in the state of Texas. I haven't forgotten a single meal of yours."

She giggled and her blue eyes sparkled. Her mass of hair was always caught up and tied behind her head with curls springing free all around her face. Madison realized that Jake hadn't seen her since her red hair had turned white. She still had her freckles and still was short, thin and wiry in spite of all her wonderful cooking.

"How have you been, Jessie Lou?" Jake asked.

"I'm fine and you look mighty fine, too."

"I do all right. How many grandkids?"

She beamed. "I have sixteen grandchildren and four great-grandchildren."

"No way—you don't look a day older."

"Then you need to see an eye doctor soon. My hair is white now."

"Prematurely, and it becomes you. Thanks for cooking dinner tonight. I can't wait and it smells marvelous."

"I'm glad you're here," she said, glancing briefly at Madison. "Now this world seems right again."

Jake grinned. "After dinner I'll tell you if you still have the magic touch in your cooking. We're searching for buried treasure, but I think the real treasure is right here in the kitchen."

She giggled and turned to stir something cooking on top of the stove.

"Would you like a cold beer or some tea or pop?" Madison asked him.

"The cold beer," he said and she retrieved one from the fridge.

"I for one would like to shower and clean up before dinner," she said. "Then I'll have a glass of wine."

"Good plan."

"I'll show you where you will stay while you're here," Madison said. "We'll be back, Jessie Lou," she stated, leading him out of the kitchen. "There's a guest suite right down the hall and my suite is upstairs." She led him into a sitting room in his guest suite.

"If you need anything, just text me. I think you'll find towels and most everything you need." She glanced down at the satchel he carried. "That's not a very big bag. If you need anything we may have some new shirts that will fit you. Look in the dresser drawers and help yourself. There aren't any extra jeans, though, and I'm afraid I can't furnish you with underwear."

"That's all right. I won't wear any," he answered. Although he didn't smile, she knew he was teasing.

"Yes, you will," she answered recklessly. "You used to wear underwear."

"Well, if you're real curious, you can always find out tonight," he said and this time there was a twinkle in his eyes and she realized she had started this. They were flirting and getting on dangerous ground. She did not want to flirt, have fun or get emotionally involved with him ever again.

"I think I started something that has to end now," she told him. "See you in the kitchen or thereabouts. If I'm not there, step outside on the patio."

"Sure," he said, giving her a curious look.

She hurried away, feeling her skin tingling. She fought the urge to turn around to see if he was still standing there watching her because she had not heard him move. She went around a corner and let out her breath. "Don't flirt with him," she whispered to herself.

She picked up a glass of ice water and went upstairs to her suite to shower and change. She swiftly washed and combed out her hair, blow-drying it and straightening it so it fell over her shoulders and down her back. She pulled on jeans, a blue knit shirt and sandals and went to the kitchen to see about the dinner that Jessie Lou was getting ready.

"Ah, you look pretty now," Jessie Lou said, smiling at her before turning back to continue stirring gravy in a pan on the gas stove.

Soon Madison heard boot heels and in seconds, Jake entered. He looked as energetic and virile as he had early this morning. When her insides clutched, she hoped she didn't have any visible reaction to the mere sight of him.

His gaze drifted over her. "You look great. You don't look as if you could have been climbing around the creek bank since sunrise."

"Thank you. I definitely feel as if I have been."

He wore a short-sleeved navy knit shirt tucked into his jeans. "It felt great to get the shower. Jessie Lou, this is the best-smelling kitchen ever. Whatever you're cooking, I can't wait."

She giggled, looking at him intently as she grinned. "I hope you like it. It's not quite ready yet."

"We'll wait until you say it's time," Jake answered as she turned back to her cooking.

Madison poured glasses of wine that they carried to the patio. They sat only ten minutes before Jessie Lou appeared. "It's on the table," she announced.

They came in to eat and Jessie Lou untied her apron. "Everything is on the table and the pie is on the counter. I'll be going now and please leave the dishes. I'll get them in the morning."

"That'll be fine. Thank you so much," Madison said.

"It was good to see you," Jake told the older woman. "And thank you for this dinner and double thanks for the pie."

Jessie Lou giggled and smiled. "You haven't eaten a bite yet."

"I know."

She giggled again and turned away, disappearing into the utility room. In minutes the back door closed and a lock clicked as she left the house.

They helped themselves to the pot roast with thick brown gravy, fluffy white rolls and creamy mashed potatoes sprinkled with tiny bits of green chives. Slender green asparagus had been steamed along with slices of carrots.

"She is still the best cook ever," Jake said as he ate. "This roast is tender and delicious."

"I have to agree," Madison said. "I'm lucky to have her because some of her children want her to come live with them."

"I would, too, if she were my mother."

"You just want a cook."

"Have you ever seen her without a smile?"

"She can get angry," Madison said, remembering when she had to tell Jessie Lou that Jake had left her on her wedding day. Jessie hadn't been smiles then and she had held Madison when she had cried, something her own mother hadn't done. Jessie Lou had kept shaking her head and repeating, "I would never have thought him to be mean like that."

Madison realized Jake was talking to her and focused on him, forgetting Jessie Lou and letting Jake charm her through dinner.

They sat on the patio until long after dark had come and the outside lights and pool lights came on automatically.

By ten o'clock, Madison was thirsty.

"Would you like iced tea, or wine, beer…or whiskey? What would you like?" Madison asked him.

"I'll just take another cold beer," he said, getting up to follow her into the kitchen. "I have some cashews we can have with our drinks," she said, standing on tiptoe, trying to reach a bowl on a high shelf. "I want this bowl—"

His hands closed on her waist to move her away. She turned abruptly.

"I'll get it," he said, but when she faced him, he inhaled and stood still. His dark gaze enveloped her and she couldn't get her breath. All she could think was that he looked as if he intended to kiss her. Her heart drummed a pounding rhythm and she couldn't move, not her hands from his arms or her eyes from his gaze. His glance lowered to her mouth and she leaned toward him. His fingers wound in her hair while his other hand slipped around her waist and pulled her against him.

The moment she pressed against him she was lost. She wanted his kiss in spite of the constant smoldering anger that flared up anytime she was reminded of the past. At that moment she couldn't move away if her life depended on it.

Desire blazed in his eyes. "Damn, Madison," he whispered, scowling. He wound his fingers in her hair and pulled slightly so she had to turn her face up.

His mouth came down on hers hard, his tongue thrust-

ing deep into her mouth and then stroking hers slowly,
teasing.

She moaned while her insides knotted with longing.
His arm tightened around her waist while he bent over
her, tasting, branding her with his possessive kiss. She
wasn't aware of wrapping her arm around his neck until
she was clinging tightly to him. He was solid, muscled,
much more so than she remembered. His kiss was stormy
and passionate. She kissed him back as if she had been
waiting for this moment since the night he'd walked out
on her, jilting her the day she had expected to be saying
her wedding vows.

When he leaned over farther, she held him tightly,
kissing him in return, unable to resist winding her fingers in his hair. Her heart pounded harder, louder, and a
moan escaped from deep in her throat. Her flesh heated,
burned, ached for his touch. The anger, the hurt and pain
and dreadful memories all were replaced by desire.

Her world narrowed until there was only this man, this
kiss. She poured herself into the kiss, taking everything
she'd missed all these years. Jake slid his mouth from hers,
hungrily nipping at her lips, her ear, her throat. Like a
dying man she gasped for air. The cool air was like a
blanket over a flame, smothering her ardor. As it rushed
into her heated lungs, she realized what she was doing.
She broke away, stepping out of his embrace and gasping for breath.

"I never meant for that to happen," she said. She ran
from him, picking up her wine and heading into the adjoining family room that overlooked the patio and pool
and gardens.

She stood looking at the blue pool, trying to get her
breath and ignore the overpowering longing that shook her.
Torn between wanting him and hating her loss of control,
she sipped the wine. She thought she was over wanting

him, beyond responding to him. His kiss shattered that illusion. She didn't want to yearn for his kisses, to ache to be held by him.

He didn't want it, either. She had heard the whispered expletive before he kissed her. Should she tell him to get out and go back to his ranch or to the bunkhouse with his men? She was tempted, but she didn't want him to know that she cared that much, that the kiss had rattled her that badly.

Making an effort to pull herself together so she could overlook and make light of the incident as if his kiss had not disturbed her and meant nothing, she took deep breaths.

She heard him moving around in the kitchen and when she turned he was standing in front of her, with his beer and the cashews in the bowl he had gotten from the cabinet.

He placed the bowl on the coffee table and they sat on opposing couches, neither speaking for a moment. She sipped her wine and tried not to watch him. She was unsuccessful. Jake looked relaxed, his long legs stretched out, crossed at his ankles. He didn't look as if he felt any inner turmoil or was racked with desire. Was he making an effort as much as she to appear indifferent or did he really feel that way?

She would never have an answer. Her insides churned. The kiss had stirred too many old feelings that she had thought were gone forever. She wanted to fling accusations at him and ask him why, but she wasn't going there. She intended to avoid a confrontation with him. She didn't want him to realize how much she still hurt over what he had done.

Instead, she talked about the fruitless search they'd endured this second day. It was the most innocuous topic she could think of. Imagine that, she thought. The generations-old feud that had involved murder and deception was a *safe* topic. But then anything that didn't involve his kiss was safe.

"I still think we're searching in the right area, but I also am aware that we could be on the wrong side of the ranch or it could be on your ranch," she said, hating the huskiness in her voice. She cleared her throat.

"That would be a hoot if both families had spent well over one hundred years searching and digging on the wrong ranch."

"It wouldn't be funny to some members of our families. Not to the ones who searched so much and so hard."

"No, it wouldn't. I hope we're not doing that."

"There's always a strong possibility that your old map and the legend, the rumors, everything might all just be a hoax."

"I have to at least try to find where they had the gunfight. That part of the story sounds like something that actually occurred." As they sat there talking about the day, she said the right words, responded to his comments in the right manner, but her errant thoughts betrayed her. Nothing could keep her mind from wandering back to the kiss. It had taken hold of her and wouldn't let her go. His kiss had opened a door that she had kept closed since high school. Desire simmered in her, but anger was bubbling inside her and she just wanted to end this night before she said things to him she shouldn't.

She stood up abruptly, cutting off what he said and she didn't hear. "I'm turning in. It's been a long day."

He stood, too, with his hands on his hips. His gaze lowered to her mouth and tingles disturbed her. She turned and left the room before her anger spilled over. Drawing in deep breaths, she reached the stairs…but there she lost the battle raging inside her. She turned and went back.

He stood much as she had left him except he was by the windows with his back to her. She wondered if he was actually looking at the pool or lost in thought.

"Jake," she said, crossing the room to stand near him

as he turned to face her. She couldn't control her fury any longer.

"I think I've waited long enough. Why did you walk out on me when we were supposed to run away and get married?"

Five

He narrowed his eyes while anger stabbed him. "Madison, you know damn well why I did. What are you up to now?"

"No, I don't know why," she snapped. "I'm not up to anything. I want an explanation."

He stared at her. As rosy spots flushed her cheeks, her fists clenched at her sides. Shock buffeted him. "I never doubted your dad for one minute. I called and you didn't answer."

"I didn't get any call from you," she said, frowning. "What are you talking about my dad? He didn't have anything to do with that night."

"The hell he didn't. And I did call you and you didn't answer."

"I was home waiting for you," she said in a strangled voice filled with anger.

"Don't put on an act with me," he snapped in disgust.

Why was she doing this now? He had never known her to lie to him.

"What I'm feeling is no act. I'm as truthful right now as I can possibly be."

"I called repeatedly and never got anyone."

"My dad? I sat beside the phone and never got a call from you. You're lying, Jake," she said, grinding out the accusation.

Fury made him shake. He closed the space between them and wound his fingers in her hair to turn her head up so he could look directly into her eyes. "Your dad told me that you had agreed you would not run away and get married. You agreed not to elope when he offered to put two hundred thousand dollars into a bank account for you and it would be your money for college and later. He offered to jump-start your art career and get you in the best galleries in Texas and on the West Coast if you would not get married."

All color drained from her face and she narrowed her eyes. But anger blazed in him, hot and ferocious, because she obviously had taken the money, later got help with her art career and agreed to what her father wanted.

"Yeah, you did," he spat out. "You wanted money more than wanting to marry me." He pulled her closer, his grip tighter on her hair. "I don't know why you started this charade, but it's a damn poor one. There's no need to dig up our past. Not now."

She jerked her head away from him. "Let me go," she snapped and he turned her loose. He strode across the room, wanting to get away from her before he said hurtful things that he'd regret. She had started this and now it was like a monster within him; he had to get away before it broke free. He reached the door before her voice stopped him.

"My dad gave me that money for college and he wanted

to help me get my art career started," Madison said stiffly. "He didn't do it to get me to call off our wedding."

Jake stopped and turned to face her again. She hadn't moved, just stood where she had been. "It didn't have anything to do with you. He told me he had opened an account for me, that he hoped I took only what I needed and perhaps a little for extras, but kept most of the money intact so I would have it when I got out of college. It had nothing to do with you or with marrying you. Absolutely nothing."

"The hell it didn't. It was a payoff. He flat out told me that he offered it to you and told you to make a choice between me or the money."

"He would never do any such thing," she said fiercely.

Pain, sharp and intense, stabbed him. Had he been bluffed by her dad? Even worse, had he been gullible enough to believe her father?

"Madison, if you're lying now—"

"I'm certainly not. Why would I? Dad gave me money for college." She frowned and stared at Jake as if she had never seen him before in her life. "My father would never hurt me that way. He wouldn't do such an underhanded thing."

Shocked, Jake stared at her. Her father had lied to him. A man who was a pillar of the community, a leader. Judge Milan had lied to him and to his daughter. And since he was regarded as so ethical and honest, he had expected to get away with the lie.

Rage made Jake clench his hands and grind his teeth. How much Pete Milan must have laughed to himself at how easily he had put that over on the two of them.

"My dad would never have hurt me like that," she repeated, her voice shaking with anger. "I don't know what you hope to gain."

"Your dad did exactly what I said he did. The judge had a reputation for honesty. Everyone in the county trusted him. I trusted him. If you're telling me the truth, I was suckered in, a gullible kid that he easily manipulated."

"I don't believe you," she said. Her fists clenched until her knuckles turned white, and the color in her cheeks now suffused her entire face. "My father would never, ever hurt me like that. He would have come to me and tried to talk me out of eloping." She shook her head as she frowned. "There's no point in going over all this. We'll finish our hunt and then I hope I never see you again," she said sharply. She spun around to hurry out of the room and he let her go.

He stood there, shock and rage warring within him alongside disbelief and acceptance. Had her dad tricked him into believing she had taken the bribe? Or would she not admit the truth—that she'd taken the money and the promise of a boost in getting her art shown instead of marriage?

If he believed her now, it would be the second time he had been taken in by a Milan. No, he wasn't going to accept her explanation. It had been a payoff, pure and simple. She had to have known the conditions and agreed to them. How else would she have not figured out what her dad was up to?

Jake's fists clenched until he realized what he was doing and opened his hands. If only they could find the treasure, the bones and the deed. He would be happy to flash the deed in her face and take her land from her.

He strode to the suite she had given him and slammed the door, standing in the center of the living area to take in deep breaths and blow them out. He had to get out and move, to work off his fury and frustration.

He left again, heading outside to jog down the ranch road toward the highway. He swore quietly when the back gate stuck and made a mental note to repair it when it was daylight.

Though he jogged faster, the memories of that fateful night caught up with him. In his mind he relived the painful hours when he'd called her repeatedly and no one had answered until he finally gave up and stopped calling. "She's lying," he mumbled to himself. Why hadn't she answered the phone if she had been so innocent?

Darkness enveloped him even though the moon shone bright. She had to know that she couldn't hide the truth or keep saying that he had never called her.

When he ran back to the ranch after his third circuit to the highway, he returned to his suite to shower. Afterward he hurried to the library to spread out the maps and papers to look again for a likely place for the hidden treasure and deed. One thing was certain: he would never get another chance to search after this one.

If he found a deed to part of her ranch, it would help ease his anger and regrets. No matter what happened, he would never be able to forget her.

Jake looked on the new day as another day of opportunity. He dressed quickly and left his room.

As he entered the front hall, tempting smells of hot bread and steaming coffee enticed him. He followed the scents into the kitchen and saw her seated in the breakfast area, with her back to him. He looked her over, taking in the snug jeans that fit her sexy backside and long legs. She wore her brown boots and a long-sleeved green shirt. Her hair was in a ponytail, tied with a green scarf, and he remembered when she had worn ponytails as a high school cheerleader.

Helping himself, he carried his plate of scrambled eggs with fresh basil, toast and a bowl of berries to the breakfast area. "May I join you?"

"I'm finished," she said, standing and picking up her plate that still had a lot of food on it. "Here's the paper."

He caught her wrist. She stopped instantly, her eyes narrowing. "What?"

"Let's try to get through the rest of this week in a civil manner the way it has been between us. Then we'll go our separate ways and probably avoid seeing each other for years again." He wanted to stand, move close and be more commanding in his request because his patience was frayed and she was obviously holding her temper in check.

"Of course," she said, jerking free, but annoying him because he would have released her anyway.

He watched her hips as she left the room until he realized what he was doing and looked away. Why did she still attract him? After last night he didn't want to be around her, yet physically, he was as attracted to her as he had been when he had been an eighteen-year-old the year they started dating.

Memories tugged at him of her leading cheers, dancing and jumping, turning flips, smiling with her ponytail swinging behind her or bouncing with each step. He had been so in love, he wouldn't have thought he would ever get over wanting her. Now all he felt was anger and lust.

He ate in silence, looking at the paper, but still lost in thought about her. When it was almost time to leave, he got up, chastising himself. There should be only one thought in his head. Finding that deed.

Madison came down the stairs and saw Jake getting ready. His brown wide-brimmed hat was squarely on his head, his gloves were half tucked into his hip pocket next to the pocketknife she knew he always carried. She walked in silence beside him until they reached the back door. As she started to punch in the code for the alarm, Jake stepped in front of her to block her.

Furious, she lashed out at him, "What do you think you're doing?"

Jake stood too close, his proximity disturbing her. Her heart raced and in spite of all the anger she felt, there still was a running current of awareness of him as an appealing man. How could she be furious with him and want him so badly?

More than ever, he towered over her, seeming inches taller than he had been when they had dated. In spite of his appeal, she wanted to get away from him and never see him again. She wanted him out of her life so she could forget him forever, instead of being in constant turmoil and having a reaction to his mere presence.

"Before you spend much time being even angrier with me than before, why don't you ask your dad what ultimatum he gave me? Just ask him what he told me you had agreed to do. While you're at it, ask him what threats he made, too."

She shook with anger and clenched her fists. "You're saying my father threatened you with physical harm?"

"No, more like financial problems. He had the power. You ask him what threats he made. And you should know me well enough to know that I would never make any such statements to you if they weren't true. I've never lied to you, Madison," he said, his dark brown eyes holding fiery anger that seemed to match what she felt.

She glared back at him another few tense seconds before he stepped away. She punched in the alarm and as he reached around her to open the door, she stepped outside without looking back. Adding to her anger, she had been aware of brushing her shoulder against him, of his arm almost touching her as he held the door.

She climbed into her truck and watched him walk to his in his long-legged stride that covered the ground swiftly. He was a tall, handsome rancher, his boots adding to his height. He was also a powerful energy mogul from an old-moneyed family. There was no way her father could have done anything to really hurt him financially.

When everyone was ready to go, she took the lead again. It was an effort to think about the coming day and searching for a buried treasure that most likely did not exist. She wanted this search to be over and done and was tempted to give it up now, tell him to get off her land and let it go.

He would accuse her of giving her word and permission and then backing out of it because of spite. He'd be right, and she didn't want to stoop to spite. His confrontation before they had left her house worried and shook her. Jake had never lied to her until that night, when he hadn't shown up after asking her to elope with him.

Otherwise, he had always been honest with her, and she had always trusted him. Her father had kept his bargain— from the time of her college graduation, she had risen to prominence in the Western art world, having showings in the most ideal galleries for her work and then opening her own successful galleries. She had a name and a following early in her career. If Jake was telling the truth, she had achieved it all at the cost of the love of her life.

She couldn't believe her father would ever stoop to doing what Jake accused him of. Never. He was a judge, had been a banker, was trusted and respected by family, friends and people from all over the state of Texas. There was no way he could have done what Jake had said. Her insides churned. How could Jake accuse her father of doing those things and then tell her to ask her father?

Maybe Jake was counting on the fact that he knew she would not ask her dad.

Then again, if there was no truth in what Jake said, he wouldn't push her to quiz her father.

The more she thought about it, the more concerned she became. She looked in the rearview mirror and saw Jake at the wheel of the truck behind her. Was he telling the truth? Knowledge of her father made her say no to her question instantly. Knowledge of Jake yielded an affirmative answer. Lost in thought, she hit a rock and the truck bounced badly. "Sorry," she said to Stoney and Darren, her passengers.

Embarrassed, she glanced in the rearview mirror to see Jake avoid the rock.

When they reached the place where they would leave the trucks, she retrieved her hat and her backpack, and turned to face Jake, who approached her. He had left the motor running in his truck and the door open and she wondered why.

"I studied the maps again last night and there's another place I want to look that isn't far from here, in an arroyo that may no longer exist. I'll go by myself so as to not waste everyone's time, but I thought you might want to send one of your hands with me."

All the time he talked, she looked at his lips and remembered his kisses. Realizing what she had been doing, she looked away.

"Stoney, do you mind going with him?"

"'Course not. Be glad to. Maybe I can help."

"I'll show you the map and what we're looking for," Jake said as the two men walked away.

She wondered how late he had sat up studying the map and if he had been unable to sleep because of the harsh words said between them. As she retrieved a shovel from the truck, she glanced back to see Jake turn around to head back the way they had come and she wondered where he was going. She would ask Stoney tonight.

The men who worked for her had been with them for a long time and were as familiar with the ranch as she was.

She wouldn't have a chance this week to go to Dallas to see her parents. It would have to be next week when the search was over and Jake and his men went back to the Calhoun ranch. Not by any stretch could she imagine her father threatening Jake. She couldn't imagine a threat that Jake would have responded to at nineteen. It all was impossible, but she had to know and the sooner, the better.

She realized she was supposed to lead the way and without Jake she would have to give everyone orders, including the men from his ranch.

She tried to focus on where she had intended to start digging today and realized she must have walked right past the place because she had been so lost in thought over Jake.

Embarrassed, she stopped to look around and turned to Darren. "Sorry, but I think we have to turn back. I think I've passed where we should start digging today."

"Whatever you say. We'll follow you."

Feeling the heat rise in her cheeks, she headed back to walk toward where they had parked. In minutes she held up her hand and everyone stopped.

"This is the area for today and all of you have a rough map of where you'll look."

The men fanned out to where each one thought he was supposed to search. She studied the copy of the map she had marked and moved closer to the creek. She began to dig and in seconds Russ, one of Jake's men, blocked her way. Pausing, she looked up at him.

Stocky with sandy hair that seemed to be swallowed up by his oversize hat, Russ faced her. "Ms. Milan, you don't need to dig. We'll do that."

"I can dig with the rest of you."

He shook his head. "My boss will have my neck if I let you dig. May I use your shovel?"

She didn't want to argue with him because his intentions were nice and she didn't want him in trouble with Jake, although at this point, she didn't care for Jake to have any say about how she lived her life. Handing Russ her shovel, she walked over to start moving away a pile of river rocks.

She watched Russ dig swiftly, moving more dirt faster than she had been able to do. She really wanted to find the treasure, the bones and be done with this.

If they didn't find the treasure and bones, Jake would never be satisfied and she could imagine that he would think she would continue searching without him after this week or two.

By the end of the day, she was exhausted. She had moved smaller rocks so others could dig, trying to concentrate on the physical labor and forget the fight with Jake. By quitting time, she was worn out. When her cell phone jingled and she heard Jake's voice, her heartbeat quickened. She still reacted physically to him in the same manner she had before their fight.

"Ready to head back?" he asked. "It'll be dark before we get there."

"Yes. We're leaving now. We'll meet you at the house."

He clicked off without a goodbye. She didn't want to spend the evening with him and intended to get something to eat and take it upstairs. At some point in the course of the day she'd made the decision to drive to Dallas tomorrow and talk to her father so she could settle this once and for all.

She refused to contemplate how it would be if Jake had been truthful. She had believed, loved and relied on her dad all her life. Her parents had done so much for her, she couldn't imagine her father doing anything to hurt her and to threaten Jake.

When they arrived at the house she went inside without waiting for him. She didn't want to be with him another minute. Nor did she want to hear about his day. If he had found anything significant, he would have told her or Stoney would have.

When she reached the back gate, the latch stuck. Determined, she jiggled it and tugged at it. He came up beside her. "Let me try," he said.

"I can't remember to have that fixed. We can go to a side door."

"I'll fix it as soon as I can. In the meantime—" He jumped over the fence, clearing the gate and landing on the other side. Before she realized what he intended, he turned, his hands closing on her waist, and he lifted her up and over the gate easily.

She grabbed his upper arms, feeling the flex of solid biceps. Startled, she looked at him and he gazed back into her eyes and the moment changed. The anger and arguments no longer held meaning. For an instant, he held her, and as she clung to him, she remembered his kisses while sparks ignited her desire.

Setting her on her feet, he released her, leaving her bereft. "I'll fix that damn latch," he said, heading for the house.

"Jake, wait," she called as she caught up with him. "I'll get Terry to fix the gate. I'll call him tonight."

"Forget it. I'll do it after dinner when it's cooler." They walked toward the back door together.

"Jessie Lou said she left dinner in the oven. Whenever you eat, you can just put any leftovers back in the oven." She wanted to make it clear she didn't intend to eat dinner with him.

"Fine," he said, holding the door for her after she unlocked it. As she switched off the alarm, he passed her.

"Jake," she called. When he turned around she said, "I'm going to skip the search tomorrow. All of you can go ahead. I'll be in touch by cell phone."

"Going to Dallas?" he asked, looking down at her.

Surprised he had so easily guessed she wanted to talk to her father, she nodded. "Yes. I want to know the truth. The trip will take most of the day."

"We'll get along and your hands will be with us so they can report back to you on everything we do," he said in a tone dripping with sarcasm. He started to walk away and then he paused. "You can fly in my jet. I'll tell my pilot. It'll save you the long drive there and back."

"Thank you, but I can drive," she said, wanting to avoid letting him do anything for her.

"Don't be ridiculous. This is no trouble. What time do you want to leave?"

"About nine in the morning," she said after a moment's hesitation, deciding it was silly to turn down his offer when it would save her hours of driving. "I'll have to see him after his work and I want to stop to see my brother because I haven't seen Nick for a while."

"Going to see the politician, Representative Milan. How's he getting along?"

"Nick keeps really busy. It's been hard for him losing Karen and the baby. They were both so excited over the prospect of a baby."

"Yeah. It was a drunk driver if I remember reading about it."

"Yes. All three were killed. After the accident Nick poured himself into politics and he's more interested in Washington now than he was before."

"What about Wyatt and Tony? More political aspirations?"

"Not at all. Until the town gets full rights in 2015 to the Lavita Wrenville house, Wyatt will stay sheriff of Verity County. Sometime in the not too distant future, Wyatt will return to ranching."

"And Tony got a law degree, didn't he?"

"Of course, but no one will pry Tony off the ranch. He hung a shingle out at the ranch for one year to pacify Mom and Dad and then tossed it aside. He said that should take care of the family superstitions."

One of Jake's dark eyebrows arched higher. "How so?"

"You've forgotten. We not only have the legend of the buried gold at the family ranch, but there's an old Milan legend that all male Milans have to go into the field of law or be doomed. They've all gone to law school."

Jake shook his head. "That's superstition. No one's doomed if they don't get into the field of law, practicing or enforcing it or, I suppose in Nick's case, creating laws. I can't imagine they are doomed if they choose another profession."

"That's what Tony thinks."

"So now you have what—four lawyers in your immediate family? One is a judge. One is a sheriff. One is a legislator, a representative to the Texas legislature, and one is a retired lawyer after one year of practice who is a rancher and does the rodeo circuit. One out of five couldn't stand the law profession—that's not bad."

"My dad loves being a judge. Ditto Wyatt being a sheriff. He's a natural for that job. I'm sure Nick will be in Washington, someday, but he would like nothing better than to be a full-time rancher."

"I can understand how he feels," Jake said.

"Tony makes no bones about it. My grandmother, Mom and Dad, Nick, they all browbeat him into getting that law degree. He has a double major—law and animal husbandry. He spent one year satisfying those members of the family and that's the last he's opened a law book or anything else regarding law unless he's had to for his ranch business. He is one hundred percent cowboy."

"I envy him."

"Anyway, I'd like to see Nick, maybe have lunch with him and go spend some time with Mom before Dad gets home," she said, realizing her anger was fading slightly the longer she stood and talked with Jake.

"Drive to the airport in Verity and get the flight there. A limo will be waiting when you get to Dallas."

"Thanks."

He shrugged.

She still didn't want to eat with him. If he had lied in any manner about her dad, she would stop this search for treasure and tell Jake to get off the ranch and not return. She suspected each one had his own version of the story, but if Jake had lied, she didn't want to deal with him five more minutes. She couldn't imagine he was right, but the nagging doubt persisted because he had been convincing.

Washing her hands, she got her dinner, serving herself to a pot of steaming chili and tamales, taking only one tamale and covering it with a little chili. She had lost her appetite. She poured ice water and carried her dinner to the study, closing the door to avoid Jake and eat alone.

First, she phoned her parents and talked to her mother before talking to her dad to ask if they would be home late tomorrow afternoon. Her mother was eager to see her and told her to stay as long as she could.

Next she called her brother Nick and they agreed to meet for lunch. She hurt for him when she broke the connection. It had been almost two years since the car wreck, but the loss was not one Nick could ever completely get over.

Madison carried her dishes to the kitchen and was relieved to see Jake wasn't there.

Would she regret learning the truth? Either way, she would be hurt and angry.

It would be another sleepless night, but by this time tomorrow, she would have some answers to her questions about Jake.

Six

She entered the kitchen by seven and Jessie Lou turned to greet her, her eyes filled with curiosity. "Jake has already left for today."

"I'm going to Dallas to see my folks today."

"Ahh. That will be good," Jessie Lou said and turned back to the pie crust she was making.

Madison stared at Jessie Lou, realizing while she kept quiet and in the background, she saw and heard a lot.

"Jessie Lou, Jake told me he didn't walk out on me on our wedding day because he didn't want to marry me. He said he was told to."

With deliberation Jessie Lou washed her hands, dried them and then turned to face Madison. For once, the woman had lost her smile. "Then it probably is time for you to find out the truth."

"Do you know it?" Madison asked because she had always felt as close to Jessie Lou in some ways as she did her mother.

"No, I don't. I've just always wondered. I think it's good that you go."

Jessie Lou's answer shook Madison because she had expected to have the cook tell her she was being foolish to even think about questioning her parents.

"I can't believe my dad would do anything to hurt me," Madison whispered, but Jessie Lou heard her.

"Well, it's time you know. You and Jake were very young. Very young."

"You do know something."

Jessie Lou shook her head. "No. I would have told you as badly as you were hurt. Maybe not right away, but I never would have waited all these years and let the hurt fester in you the way it has. I see the way the two of you look at each other. It's time the truth comes out."

"I can't believe it."

"It's best to go ask because now you'll wonder until you do." She turned back to the pie crust.

Madison had lost her appetite and carried her dishes to the counter. Jessie Lou looked at her. "Are you all right?"

Madison nodded. "I think so. I'm going to get ready to go. Jake is letting me fly in his plane. His pilot will be waiting."

Jessie Lou nodded. "I will be thinking about you— both of you."

Feeling far more worried, Madison left to get dressed.

At eleven, she rode in a limo to a restaurant in Dallas where she told the driver she would call him when she needed him again. She hurried inside the glass-enclosed round building. In the lobby Nick stepped up to greet her and give her a light hug. Three inches over six feet tall, Nick oozed personality. He was a politician through and through and she had heard their dad talk to Nick about a presidential run someday. She couldn't imagine, yet Nick had won every race he had entered from Most Popular Boy in the Sixth Grade to his reelection to the Texas legislature.

Gold cuff links complemented his tailor-made white shirt. He wore a brown suit and a dark brown tie. Whether it was a working day or not, Nick was always camera-ready.

His dark brown hair was the color of hers and his eyes were blue. There the similarity ended because his face was longer, his hair wavy, his nose had a slight crook from being broken playing football in a neighborhood game. Nick had perfect, snowy teeth, along with a smile that probably helped him win votes. People had always liked him and he seemed full of life, able to enjoy himself more than most people. Every day was an adventure for him and she had often been amazed by his perpetual optimism and energy. He had changed after the loss of his pregnant wife and their baby, but to her relief his cheerfulness was beginning to return to him.

Hugging her, Nick smiled as he stepped away. "Thanks for calling. I'm glad to see you. I've got a table waiting."

They looked at their menus briefly, ordered, and while they waited, he smiled again. "I saw you drive up. So what's the deal with the limo? The art must be doing extremely well."

"Jake Calhoun let me fly in his private jet today and he arranged for the limo. That's his chauffeur."

"After the heartbreak Jake caused you, I don't see why you agreed to let him search on your ranch."

"I still think of it as the family ranch, even though Dad has put it in my name. It would benefit us, too, if Jake finds anything. Today, some of our men are with him, so he's not out there looking without Milan interests being protected. And I've gone with them every day until today."

"When we were at Verity High, I liked Jake, but after

what he did to you, I haven't trusted him or wanted to be around him or have any dealings with him."

"Sounds funny, coming from you, because you're always friendly to him," she said, unable to argue with him. "You're always friendly with everyone,"

He grinned. "I want to keep those votes coming." His smile vanished. "Kidding aside, you said he's giving you the treasure if you find it—I think that's suspicious. Why is he being so generous? I don't believe for a second he's interested in his ancestors' remains. It's not like remains that need to be returned to a sacred tribal burial ground."

"I told you he's hoping to find a deed giving him a bit of the McCracken ranchland."

"Sounds fishy to me, Madison." He shook his head, unconvinced. "Be careful. If you find remains, you won't know whose they are. Could have been a posse after a Milan or a Calhoun."

"Well, if we find bones, we'll get a forensic specialist to identify them and any Milan bones will get a proper burial in our Milan cemetery."

Nick's blue eyes rested intently on her. "Keep me posted and watch Jake. I wouldn't trust him one second."

"I will. How are you doing, Nick?" she asked, suddenly eager to change the subject.

"Busier than ever," he replied. "People are sounding me out about running for a U.S. Senate seat."

"That would be fantastic. I'm thrilled for you," she said and for an instant saw a slight frown crease his brow, but then it was gone. "You don't want to do that?"

"We're a long, long way from me having to make that decision, but yes, I'd like to. In a way, I hate to get so far from Texas and the ranch, but politics is my life and if I really get a chance for this, I'm taking it."

"Of course you should," she said. "Your life revolves around politics." While they were served, they remained silent. She watched as a tossed salad was placed in front of her and then a waiter placed a hamburger in front of Nick.

"Do the folks know you're letting Jake dig on the ranch?"

"Of course. Someone, maybe Charley, keeps Dad posted and Dad has already called to try to talk me out of letting Jake search. So far it's been as useless and hopeless as when y'all dug for that treasure when you were kids."

Nick grinned. "We imagined finding a big trunk filled with gold. We never gave a thought to ancestors' bones and knew nothing about a deed."

"We'll see. You can always come join us."

He laughed and she smiled because she knew his schedule kept him busy every minute, which was what he wanted. She was certain he was trying to occupy his time so he wouldn't have a chance to think too much about his loss.

She chatted and ate, finishing and sipping iced tea until Nick glanced at his watch. "I'm sorry. I have to get back to the office. I have an appointment."

"It's been good to see you. I need to call the limo," she said as they stood to walk out. She put away her phone. "He's already here and waiting. Want a lift back to your office?"

"No, thanks. I drove myself." Nick smiled at her. "Thanks for having lunch with me."

"Thanks for taking me," she replied. "You take care of yourself, Nick."

"You, too. See you soon," he said.

He followed her until they were almost at the limo. "Shall I tell the chauffeur to drive carefully?"

She grinned. "You? My brother who got into trouble for drag racing?"

He laughed and shrugged. "I'm grown up and responsible now." He smiled at her and walked away as she climbed into the limo for the ride to their parents' home.

It wasn't too long until they reached the gated community where mansions started above one million in price. The well-landscaped grounds had tall oak trees along the wide, winding drive to the house while giant magnolias grew between the oaks.

Like the house on their family ranch, this was another Georgian redbrick with white Corinthian columns. Two beds of red and yellow hibiscus bloomed on either side of the front porch. She used her key to unlock the front door. A small shaggy brown dog stood in the foyer wagging its tail.

She hurried inside, stopping to pet the happy dog. "Hi, Prissy," Madison said, scratching the dog's head. "Where's your family?"

The little dog danced around her as Madison searched for her parents, finding them in the study, her father playing with another brown dog, her mother holding a laptop. The moment she saw Madison, she smiled and came forward to hug her.

Catching a whiff of her mother's rose perfume that she had worn as long as Madison could remember, Madison felt foolish for even coming because she couldn't imagine that her father had done anything to hurt her or that her mother would allow him to.

Even after the hug, her mother's beige silk blouse and matching silk slacks did not have a wrinkle. Madison had always thought her mother was a beautiful woman and at fifty-two, Evelyn Milan still looked beautiful to Madison. Her short brown hair was perfectly styled.

"Well, look who's here," her dad said as he came to hug her. Twelve years older than her mother, her dad's life revolved around law and being a judge. Even in his aged brown slacks, a white dress shirt and a favorite brown cardigan he looked imposing and judicial. He had never had to raise his voice to get Madison or Nick or Wyatt to obey him when they had been children. Only Tony had been the wild one who could sometimes wear their father's patience to the breaking point.

Madison kissed both parents and sat to talk to them, bringing them up to date on the search for the buried treasure. Her father sat listening quietly, which she knew meant he was thinking.

"I've always heard about the gun battle and that members of both families were killed," he said, "so it's logical their bones are out there somewhere if they weren't carried off by animals."

"Pete, that's gruesome," Evelyn Milan said, shivering.

"It's the truth. I can imagine someone from each family returning to bury their own dead. That part of the tale I've always thought was true. As for a buried treasure—who knows? Could have been or might be pure myth. It might be as little as two or three gold coins. And he didn't ask you to split the booty with him?"

Madison shook her head. "No, sir. He said he didn't want the treasure, whatever it is, just his ancestors' bones."

"That's generous," Evelyn said.

"I don't think he believes there is really any treasure and it's an inducement to get me to agree to this," Madison explained.

"That makes sense," Pete said. "I imagine he's done plenty of looking on his side of the boundary when he was a kid. Besides, you said there might be a deed giving the Calhouns some McCracken land?"

"Yes, that's what Jake is hoping to find," she replied.

"Madison, be careful. I don't trust the Calhouns. There may be more to this than we know."

"I know he wants to lease the land and he wants the mineral rights. I think he intends to drill gas wells. I've gotten several calls from energy companies, geologists. I told you a while back, Dad, for right now, I'm talking to three companies to see which one will be the best deal for us. None of them belong to Jake. I'll let you know before I do anything. I want you to approve."

"Thanks, that's very nice, Madison. I'm sure Mom and I will be happy with whatever you decide."

"I don't know that I'll make any decisions before your trip, but I'll keep you in the loop." Her parents were leaving in November to go to Paris, Switzerland and the Italian coast. Her aunt Edna was staying at the house to watch the dogs. "Is there anything I can do while you're gone?"

"Thank you, but no, Madison," her mother answered. "If there is, we'll let you know."

"You should have a wonderful trip." They spent the next half hour talking about the upcoming vacation and their plans.

"Mom, I have a legal problem I need to discuss with Dad. Would you excuse us? I think this will bore you terribly."

"Of course. And you're right—I don't need to hear a legal problem unless *you're* in trouble with the law."

Smiling, Madison shook her head. "Hardly. Old stuff and nothing illegal."

"I'll give you an hour and then I'll be back. That's long enough for legal talk," Evelyn said as she left the room, taking the dog with her. Madison followed her to the door.

"Thanks, Mom. I'll come get you," she said, closing the door after her mother had walked away. She walked back across the room to face her dad.

He sat in his favorite chair with his feet propped on an ottoman, his feet crossed at the ankles. He looked relaxed, friendly, supportive, but a glance into his alert blue eyes and she knew he was paying attention and ready to listen.

She wanted to catch him off guard, hoping to be able

to tell by looking at him if he had been honest in what he had said to Jake.

She pulled a wingback chair close to the ottoman to face him.

"What's happened, Madison?" he asked.

She leaned forward, placing her hands on his knees. "Dad, when I was in high school, I was going to elope with Jake Calhoun. He never showed up. Why?" Her heart pounded hard. She had never questioned her father before. As a child she had thought every word he said was the absolute truth and the way things should be. She had always obeyed, never rebelled; when he wanted her to do something, she had always done it unquestioningly.

His expression never changed. There was not even a flicker of an eyelid, yet she knew something was wrong. Her dad had waited too long to reply. She couldn't get her breath and her head swam.

Jake had been telling the truth.

She gulped for air.

"Madison, are you all right? Do you need to lie down?"

She shook her head, but she couldn't get her breath. She closed her eyes and held her head in her hands, gulping for air while her whole world shifted and changed.

The father she had always implicitly trusted had deceived and hurt her. Jake had walked out because of her father.

"Dad, how could you have done that to me?" she said between her gasps for air. Jake had been right. That was all she could think. And she hadn't believed him at all. "I didn't think you would ever hurt me like that," she whispered, staring at him while hot tears spilled from her eyes.

"Madison, I love you and I did it for you. You were way too young to get married then."

"There were so many other ways to handle it that wouldn't have hurt us that badly." Her father's betrayal had caused a lasting hurt that might be with her all her life. "I've been so awful to Jake and accused him of terrible things."

"First of all, he's a Calhoun and this family would never accept him. His family wouldn't accept you. Second, both of you were children and you were way too young and immature to go into marriage. I see too much suffering and unhappiness. I couldn't let you throw away your future."

"Why didn't you talk to me? I've always done what you wanted."

"You have, but you were growing up and getting more headstrong. Your elopement would have divided both families and brought that old feud back to life, stronger than it had been in over a century. Those who sided with you and were ready to end the feud would have split with those who would have opposed you and felt you betrayed your family. Some family members would never have recognized you as part of the family again."

"Did you physically threaten Jake?"

"I did bring some pressure to bear because Jake would understand that kind of threat."

Shock gripped her as she stared in silence.

"Honey, I'm sorry. Maybe you and Jake would have worked things out and been happy the rest of your lives, but the odds were not on your side. And neither of you had your education completed. You hadn't even finished high school."

"I don't know you. I don't know how you could have threatened Jake and gone behind my back to be cruel and deceitful," she said, feeling her pride in him and her high regard for him crumble.

"I wasn't exactly happy about it, but I had to stop both of you. I didn't even know you were seeing each other until Charley saw you climbing out and leaving the ranch. I started asking quietly and it didn't take long to find out."

She covered her eyes and cried quietly. "What you did was so awful and hurt badly all these years." She looked at him. "I've always trusted you totally, but I never will again."

"I hope you do. I hope you fall in love and marry, and if you do and have your own children, you will see that in life you have to make tough decisions. I know few people who haven't had to face them with their children. Then maybe you'll understand."

"I'll never understand you threatening Jake. I can't understand you being underhanded. If you had come to me and said we couldn't marry, I would have argued, but I wouldn't feel this dreadful deceit. If you had said, 'You can't elope. I'll annul it,' you know I would have done what you wanted even though I wouldn't have liked it."

"You might have, but Jake wouldn't have been so obedient to me, a Milan. Besides, I didn't know how much influence he carried with you. Honey, I apologize," he said. "Maybe I didn't handle it right. But babies don't come into the world with instructions on how to raise them, you know."

"I sat by the phone all that afternoon and evening and Jake never called, but he told me he called repeatedly. Why didn't I get his calls?" she asked, ignoring his apology that came way too late and only because she asked.

He looked away and ran a hand through his hair. "It was the weekend. I had the calls forwarded to the line in my toolshed. It simply rang and no one answered. On Monday I switched it back."

"Did Mom know?"

"Partly. She didn't want you to marry a Calhoun and she wanted me to stop you. She didn't know exactly how I did so." He looked at her, and his shoulders somehow didn't seem quite so broad. "I'll call Jake and I'll try to talk to him. Being a Calhoun, he will probably always hate me and I may have added years to this archaic feud."

She tried to take in her father's explanation, painful though it was. But one thing didn't make sense. "I didn't get him when I called him. You couldn't change his phone."

"That was the one thing I worried about, but by the time you tried to call him, he had already left town. I knew his folks were out of town that weekend and all his siblings were furious with you."

He sat forward and reached out for her, but she pulled back. "I'm sorry, Madison, but I still feel it was for the best, and at this point in your life, I'd think you'd agree. You have a marvelous career in art, a field that is difficult and competitive. You and Jake are free to marry now and if you don't want to now, my guess is that a marriage at sixteen and nineteen would not have lasted anyway."

"If I had called him right after talking to you, I might have learned the truth."

"It was a chance I had to take. But I thought I'd made him so angry with you, that he wouldn't have taken your call or believed anything you said. I'm amazed he tried to call you. If you had gotten through, then I would have tried other ways to stop you and I would have called his parents to intervene. I don't think the two of you could have fought both families."

Each revelation made her pain deepen. "All these years I thought he just left me waiting with no explanation," she said, thinking about Jake and the intervening years.

"Jake went home, packed and left for college that afternoon, way, way early. I had someone check on him."

She fished a tissue from her pocket and wiped her eyes, standing and turning away from him. The tears wouldn't stop. When she thought how furious she had been with Jake all these years, her stomach churned.

"Dad, for thirteen years I have been angry with Jake.

I've shed a million tears over his walking out on me. I married someone I didn't love just to get back at Jake—"

He stood in front of her. "I was afraid of that. Madison," he said, frowning and looking more worried than she had ever seen him look, "your mother and I were afraid you were doing that, but we hoped the marriage would work out and you would find happiness. Will was a nice fellow and quite acceptable to the family."

"Our marriage was dreadful."

"That's behind you now. I'll call Jake and talk to him. I owe you both that much, but if I had it to do over, I probably would do things the same way. I don't think I could have stopped the two of you otherwise."

"There had to have been better ways to handle it and you could have been honest. That's what I'm having a difficult time with." She walked away from him. "It's going to take me a while to get accustomed to all this. I would never have believed you could have done such a thing if you hadn't told me yourself."

"I apologize, Madison, and I hope someday you'll understand and you'll forgive me. But let me ask you something. Do you think you would have been the artist you are today if you had run away and married Jake?"

Startled, she turned to look at him and thought about the years and the work, the hours she had poured into her art career, especially after being so hurt.

"Maybe not, Dad, but a career doesn't trump love."

"You wouldn't have had this wonderful success," he replied solemnly.

He reached out to hug her, but she stood stiffly. He released her and stepped back. "I love you, Madison. Always remember that. I'm human and not infallible in spite of being a judge. And judges may be the worst with their own families."

From out of nowhere a thought struck her. She remembered the tree across the bridge on the ranch. "Dad, someone cut down a big cottonwood and it blocked the bridge over Rocky Creek. Did you have anything to do with that?"

He shook his head. "I don't even know where you're searching. Trust me, I haven't been out on the ranch sawing down big trees."

Before she could answer, there was a light knock at the door and the door opened. Evelyn thrust her head into the room. "Ready for company yet?"

"Sorry, Mom," Madison said. "I have to go. I should get back to the ranch so I can hear how the men did today." She cast a glance at her father. "We're finished here."

Her mother studied her intently and gave her dad a penetrating stare. Madison wanted out before her mother realized the problem and they started discussing it all over.

She felt she had to get out or suffocate. She needed fresh air and to get away by herself for a while before she went back to the ranch to face Jake when he returned tonight. Jake had been right all along. She hurt all over for what her dad had done. She felt betrayed, hurt and filled with regret. She owed Jake an enormous apology.

Her folks followed her out to hug her before she left. When her dad hugged her, he brushed her cheek with a kiss. "You just remember always that I love you. That's always my motivation."

She nodded and turned away.

"Madison," her dad said and she paused to turn back. "Be careful. I don't think Jake can really care that much about his ancestors' bones. He's still a Calhoun and he's got a reason to want revenge."

"I'll be careful," she said stiffly. The chauffeur held the limo door for her and she climbed in. She didn't look back as the limo drove away. She didn't want to cry in the limo so she fought tears and emotions that rocked her.

She was still in shock, reeling and adjusting to seeing a side to her father that was tough and hard, a side she had never seen before.

Tonight she had to apologize to Jake. She thought of all his pent-up anger. He had never told her about her dad until now. What had her dad threatened to do to him that had scared Jake off? He didn't scare easily and he especially wouldn't as a nineteen-year-old. There had been something. Some kind of leverage. Her dad had been a powerful attorney back then with a lot of influence. At one time he had been with the district attorney's office before she had even started school. They were wealthy, influential. Her mother was also from an old Texas family.

At the same time, Jake's family could match them in power and wealth, and the Calhouns were an old Texas family with roots that went back to the 1800s.

It wouldn't have mattered, though. Jake would never have had any help from his own family because some of the Calhouns still hated the Milans with a vengeance. Jake's mother was one—she had never spoken to Madison or any other member of the Milan family that Madison knew about. His grandparents disliked Milans also, but she suspected the animosity worsened steadily with each previous generation. Lindsay Calhoun would not speak to any Milan and Tony's fights with Lindsay as his neighboring rancher were notorious.

Madison wanted the truth, all of it. She felt dazed, shocked that her own father had been the one to destroy her plans to marry Jake.

If she had confronted her father back then, would he have admitted what he had done?

She would never have an answer to that question.

Frowning, she stared out the limo window, but she

didn't see the surroundings. She saw Jake's angry dark eyes. His anger ran deep and now she could understand it.

They would all get in about dark and she had to be ready to face him.

The minute she entered the kitchen her eyes met Jessie Lou's and Madison was swamped by the emotional upheaval of the day. She couldn't control her feelings as tears spilled down her cheeks.

"Jessie Lou, Dad admitted everything Jake accused him of doing. All these years—" She couldn't talk. And then Jessie Lou's arms wrapped around her and she clung to Jessie Lou to cry.

"You finally know. I always thought Judge Milan might have been behind whatever happened. He's very close to Charley and Charley keeps an eye on you for your dad. Charley has never liked Jake."

Madison stepped back. "Charley? Yesterday someone cut a big cottonwood so it fell on the bridge and blocked the way. Jake and the men moved it, but it gave us a delay. Do you suppose my dad told Charley to try to interfere?"

Jessie Lou stared back with a slight frown. "I'd be careful around Charley."

Madison cried, trying to get control of her emotions. Finally she wiped her eyes. "I was just so shocked that my dad would do something like that and not be open and honest about it."

"You're his daughter. He thought he was protecting you."

"Instead, he hurt me badly and I feel terrible for the hateful way I've treated Jake all these years."

"It's over now, I'd say," Jessie Lou said. "I have dinner all fixed and I think I will go along and leave you two to discuss the past with no interference. I won't be here until after lunch tomorrow because I have a dental appointment in Lubbock in the morning, so you should have the privacy you need to talk this out."

Madison wiped her eyes and tried to smile. "Thank you. I'm going to shower and get ready. Jake will be here by dark."

Jessie Lou nodded and patted her shoulder. "You'll both be better off now that you can clear the air between you."

Madison nodded, but she wondered if they could ever get back even some of the friendship they once had. "I'll get ready for Jake."

Jake glanced at his watch as he walked toward the Milan ranch house. He was tempted to go on home, but staying here was easier and they could have slightly more time each day to hunt. The days were flying past and his options dwindled with each one. They hadn't found anything. Madison would never give him another chance so he wanted to find the deed this week.

He was hot, dusty and disgusted that they didn't know any more about a buried treasure than they had when they started. He wondered how it went with Madison and her dad. He hated Judge Milan and would be more than happy to take a big chunk of the judge's ranch from him. And if he did find treasure and a deed and got the land, he was going to go tell the judge himself. How sweet that would be. Madison had no idea how harsh her father could be or what he had really done in the past. Would Judge Milan lie to his daughter now? If he did, could Jake ever convince her otherwise? Soon they'd part again and he didn't expect to see her after they did.

Jake rang the bell at the locked back door.

In minutes the door opened and she stood in the shadowy interior. She stepped back. "Come in."

He entered and paused. Her hair was down, hanging loosely over her shoulders and framing her face in a brown cascade that was longer than he had guessed. She had on makeup and a short-sleeved hot-pink cotton dress with a scoop neck that revealed her curves and took his breath away.

"You look gorgeous," he said, his voice raspy, lust consuming him. For a few seconds he forgot where she had gone today or why or the harsh differences between them when he had last seen her in the morning.

"Come in. Would you like a beer before dinner?" she asked.

"Sure," he thought he answered. He couldn't be sure; all he could think about was how much he wanted her. He watched her walking ahead of him, saw that familiar little sway of her hips that had stirred him plenty of times and did again now.

She turned and gave him a look filled with curiosity. "Jake? Are you all right?"

"I can't stop looking at you," he admitted.

She smiled, but it was cool and brief and he had a feeling she didn't really feel like smiling, but was merely being polite. He thought about her trip to Dallas and was curious because she didn't give a hint of what had happened or what she felt.

He followed her and watched her get his beer and a tall glass of ice water for herself. He sipped and lowered the bottle.

"That's really good," he said, but he looked at her as he spoke and he was thinking about her, not his beer.

"Do you want to talk now or get cleaned up?"

It took a second for her words to register. He stared at her. She looked cool, clean, sexy. He wanted to touch her.

"I need to clean up first because I'm covered in dust. I'll be back shortly. Don't go away. Don't change."

This time she did smile. "I won't do either one. See you soon."

"You sure will," he said, hurrying out of the room. Curiosity consumed him. He couldn't read her reaction, but he was beginning to hope her father had confessed to the truth. Jake had never expected him to, but if Pete Milan had lied about what he had done, Jake didn't think Madison would have let him in her house now.

Jake lengthened his stride. He wanted to find out what had happened and how she had reacted.

Madison watched him go, thankful she'd had an effect on him. She wanted to leave him dazzled. Time was when she could do so without much effort. That was no longer true. He seemed so angry sometimes when they had been together that she had wondered if he even liked her anymore.

She had talked to Jessie Lou about dinner and she had made appetizers and dessert. Jessie Lou had great-looking steaks ready to grill so Madison hoped he liked dinner.

It was another half hour before he reappeared and now she felt desire blaze as she looked at him. His hair was neatly combed, the ends still damp near the collar of his Western shirt. His jeans hugged his strong legs.

"Do you want another beer? I have some appetizers I made. We can take our drinks and appetizers to the family room or we can sit outside."

"Beer and family room sounds good to me."

He helped as she retrieved a plate of imported cheeses and fancy crackers. They carried them to the family room and set them on a table. Dreading the next hour, but knowing it was long overdue, she turned to face him, meeting his gaze.

As Jake sipped his beer, he noticed she appeared worried with a slight frown on her brow and her fingers locked together tightly in her lap. He had a swift rush of satisfaction.

"Your dad must have admitted what he did," he said.

Standing, she faced him while her frown deepened. She shivered and stepped away as if she had to move around. In seconds her eyes met his. "Jake, I'm so sorry."

Her eyes filled with tears, but he couldn't feel sorry for her. He merely nodded. "Apology accepted, but you're not the one who should be apologizing."

"I didn't know my dad was capable of what he did. I didn't dream he would ever do such a thing as threaten you and I didn't think he would do something that would hurt me so badly. I had no inkling that he was behind your disappearance. Not a clue. Why didn't you tell me?"

"Your dad must not have confessed everything. He told me to pack and go to college early, to get away and to stay away from you. He threatened me if I didn't."

"Threatened you with what?" she asked, her voice barely above a whisper.

"He would do everything he could to ruin my future. He would try to make life difficult for me if I lived around here. He listed several possibilities. Frankly, I didn't think my family would have protected me."

Shaking her head, Madison placed her hand over her eyes. He didn't think it was an act. Madison had always been sincere with him. Tears filled her eyes and he could see her struggle for control.

"I don't even know my own dad and that's dreadful. And I know you're right—you couldn't turn to your family for help."

"No, I couldn't," he said, standing and stepping closer to face her. She wrung her hands. He was certain she wasn't even aware of what she was doing. "Some members of my family hate all Milans. They would have been as bad as your dad. I knew that at the time. We were on our own in too many ways and we got caught."

"I feel terrible that I was angry with you." The tears spilled over, running down her cheeks. "I always thought you walked out on me."

"I was angry because I thought you would rather have all he offered instead of me. We had been so in love, Madison. But he was so emphatic that it was your wish and since it was, he was warning me to leave you alone and stay far away. If I didn't, he would let my family know."

She wiped away the tears but they wet her cheeks again quickly. "Sorry. I can't control my emotions. I'm still shocked. I wouldn't have ever believed my father capable of hurting me or being so cruel if I hadn't clearly heard him admit it today. Jake, I'm just terribly sorry I've been mean to you. You didn't cause it any more than I did. I wish you had called me and told me everything."

"I couldn't get through to you, remember?"

"My dad told me about that. He had the calls sent to the phone line in his toolshed on the ranch. I never knew you tried to call."

"I can't believe I was so gullible, either." Jake shook his head. "But even if we had managed to elope, with your dad's power and influence he would have found a way to separate us and have the marriage annulled."

"You had a scholarship to play football in Mississippi. I thought if we had married, and I had gone with you, they wouldn't have brought me back." She looked at him, raising her chin.

They stared at each other and his gaze ran over her features again, sliding down to her low neckline and tempting curves. His gaze returned to her mouth. He didn't know what his feelings were for her, but he knew he wanted her. He wanted to make love to her. She was no teenage girl anymore. She was a grown, intelligent woman who could make her decisions with far more judgment and clarity.

He set his beer on a table and closed the space between them. As he approached her, her eyes widened. Her lips parted as she took a deep breath.

"Jake?" she asked breathlessly.

Seven

Jake leaned down to cover her mouth with his own. His arms tightened around her and he leaned over her.

Madison pressed against him, standing on tiptoe to kiss him passionately.

"Jake, forgive me," Madison whispered, pausing a moment.

"It's in the past, Madison," he replied. "Let it go because it's over and can't ever affect us again unless we let it."

"I was as mean to you as my dad," she said, feeling agonized as a deep frown furrowed her brow.

"Forget it now," he ordered. "You didn't know and I couldn't fight your family and mine. We wouldn't have been able to stay together because you were underage. The main thing is now you know I did not deliberately hurt you."

Madison pulled his head down to kiss him. She wanted him with all the longing that seemed to have built through the past empty years. She wanted to love him and be loved by him, mindlessly, not thinking about yesterday or tomorrow, just to love him once again for what had been taken from them. She wanted to forget and replace the past with memories of today.

She kissed him passionately, winding her fingers in his thick hair, relishing touching him, thinking he was still the most exciting man she had ever known.

While she kissed him, she leaned away a fraction to undo the buttons on his knit shirt. Her hands went to his belt and she unfastened the heavy buckle he had won in a rodeo.

With shaking fingers she tugged his shirt swiftly from his jeans. He released her to yank his shirt over his head and toss it away.

While he slid the zipper down the back of her dress, he watched her. She glanced up and the blatant desire in his brown eyes made her weak-kneed.

As she started to move closer again, he held her away. "Wait," he commanded. He slipped her dress off her shoulders and when he let it fall, she stepped out of it. His gaze roamed over her slowly, a tantalizing perusal that she knew was the precursor to his caresses. She inhaled, tingling, wanting to grab him. Instead, she clung tightly to his upper arms as he unfastened her bra and tossed it aside.

"Jake," she whispered as he cupped her breasts. His hands were warm, rough, calloused from the days of digging and moving rocks, heightening sensations as he caressed her so lightly, his thumbs circling her nipples with feathery touches that set her on fire.

She repeated his name, loving the feel of it on her mouth, just as she relished the feel of his hands on her breasts. She closed her eyes and moaned with pleasure. One hand continued to caress her while his other hand peeled away her lace panties, letting them fall around her ankles so she could step out of them.

He bent to take her nipple in his mouth, his tongue replacing his thumb and driving her wild.

She held his shoulders tightly, tension mounting, desire a raging fire, while uppermost in her mind was the knowledge that she was being loved by Jake. Nothing would ever give them back the lost years, but right now, in this moment, he was making love to her. At last, she could freely make love to him in return, to try in this way to convey her regrets and long-ago feelings for him that had remained part of her life even when he had gone.

"Jake, there's never been anyone that it's been the same with," she whispered. She opened her eyes to unfasten his jeans and push them off his narrow hips.

As her gaze ran over his chest, she inhaled deeply, wanting him with a building desperation. She didn't think she could wait as long as he could hold out and continue the foreplay that built flames into a raging inferno of need.

"I don't know how to make it up to you," she whispered, looking up at him.

His lips were red from her kisses and his eyes still filled with naked desire.

"You can keep trying," he whispered, kissing her breast and making her forget conversation.

She knelt to caress and kiss him, hoping to stir him to the heights where he had already taken her. She wanted him to remember this night, to know she had regrets and was trying to make it up to him. She wanted to make up in a tiny measure for lost years of loving between them.

His fingers tangled in her hair while she stroked and kissed him until he caught her beneath her arms and raised her to her feet. He swung her into his arms and carried her to his bedroom. Setting her on her feet beside the bed, he yanked back covers and then placed her on the cool sheets.

He stretched beside her, kissing her and caressing her while he held her. In minutes he moved over her, rolling her over and kissing her slowly, a hot torment as his tongue teased and desire built even more.

"It's been so long," she whispered.

"Too long, Maddie."

A thrill spiraled from her head to her toes. *Maddie*. That's what he had always called her before, but never once since he had been back. She wanted to hear him say it again, and again.

"Jake, make love to me. It's been so long." She pulled him to her, lost in desire, but then she remembered. "I'm not protected."

He moved away, stepping off the bed to retrieve his jeans, and came back with a package. She watched him slip on the condom, looking at his strong hands that she remembered so well.

Her gaze inched over him slowly, taking in his strong thighs with short brown hairs sprinkled over them, his thick rod that was ready, his virile body, muscled, fit and vital, energy radiating from him.

His dark brown eyes studied her as much as she studied him. Locks of his black hair fell on his forehead. He was handsome, exciting, sexy, marvelous. His kisses and lovemaking could rock her and touch the core of her being, an intimacy that she treasured.

Once, she had loved him with all her heart. So much had happened between them and she had harbored bitter feelings for so long, she didn't know what she felt now except passion and lust. She wanted his hard body against her, his thick manhood inside her, filling her, driving her over a blinding edge.

"Jake, let's make love," she whispered again.

"We are, darlin'. Maddie, you're the most beautiful, exciting woman I've ever known," he whispered and came down to cover her mouth with his before she could answer him. He entered her slowly, driving her wild as he pulled away for seconds and then claimed her again.

She held him tightly while she kissed him possessively, thrusting her tongue deep over his and clinging to him.

He eased into her and withdrew slowly, setting her on fire and then repeating his thrusts. Her hips arched against him, her legs pulling him closer as they wrapped around his narrow waist and held him tightly.

Sweat dotted his forehead as he continued to move with slow deliberation, holding off while building her need, until she didn't know what she was saying to him, what she was feeling except the desire to cling tighter, move faster.

When his control snapped, he thrust quickly and she rocked with him, rising and crashing over the edge. She cried out with eagerness, climaxing in a release that dazzled her.

Rapture spilled over her along with joy because he was in her arms, loving her and sharing the most intimate moments. He shuddered and pumped with his own release, gasping for breath.

Afterward, he showered kisses on her, making her wonder if he truly felt such closeness and tenderness for her or if it was merely a response to his own satisfaction.

In some ways now, she felt she knew so little about him. They had grown up and been apart all these years. They had both lived in anger and bitterness toward the other, so she didn't have the closeness with him that they had shared as kids.

She stroked his damp back, running her fingers along the strong column of his neck and then through his hair. She held him to her, welcoming his weight, his closeness.

He rolled to his side, taking her with him, and he smiled at her while he held her. "This is the best, Maddie."

Another thrill rocked her. She liked having him go back to the old nickname that only he had ever called her. "It seems right to be together and in some ways it wipes out the empty years between then and now," she said.

"Your dad cheated us of a lot of time together. No one will ever know if he was right or not and I suppose if I had a sixteen-year-old daughter, I might stop her from marrying, too. That's young, Maddie, even though we didn't feel it at the time."

"We'll never know, Jake. If we had married then, we'd probably have four or five kids by now and I wouldn't have had an art career."

"It's in the past. There's no use speculating and thinking about the 'what ifs.'"

She gazed beyond him, thinking about what he just said, to forget their love and their times together and what they had planned. Had tonight been purely lust for both of them? What did she really feel for him and what did Jake feel for her?

She couldn't answer her questions, but she suspected that he was no longer in love. They were basically strangers now. Sadness filled her and she ran her hands over him, unable to get enough of touching him. The memories of making love long ago were to a different person—a boy. Now he was a man and physically, as well in other ways, he had changed. She had, too. Maybe what they once had had been lost forever.

She tightened her arms around him and pressed against him, holding him tightly. For right now, she was satisfied. They had shared a closeness that was good and the anger and bitterness between them no longer existed. That had to be better.

"You used to talk more than you do now," she remarked.

He smiled, twisting to look at her. "Another change. I've been alone so long, maybe in some ways, I'm all locked up inside myself. I still say life has changed. Just keep on with taking one day at a time."

They both became silent and she wondered what thoughts ran through his mind. Had too much bitterness passed between them for them to rekindle a relationship?

Physically, it would be no problem, but there was far more to it than a physical relationship. They had lost the joy they once shared. She remembered her father's warning to be cautious about Jake, that he might want more from this treasure hunt than he had indicated.

At the thought of her father, she recalled her afternoon visit with him.

"It won't mean anything to you," she told Jake, "but my dad apologized to me for what he did."

"That's nice for you, but it doesn't change a thing."

"I know, but I'm glad he did and glad he feels some remorse."

Jake toyed with her hair and remained silent. "You're a beautiful woman."

"Thank you."

They gazed into each other's eyes. Desire stirred and he leaned closer, his gaze drifting to her mouth. She couldn't get her breath. She wanted his kiss, needed him just as if they had never made love. She turned her face up to him and then raised her lips to kiss him.

His arms tightened around her and he turned on his back, pulling her on top of him. Her hair fell around her face as she kissed him and passion rekindled.

It was like that throughout the night. He held her in his arms and they made love often, as if they could never get enough of each other.

In the morning he worshipped her body once again, then, afterward, he held her close. "Shall we call off the search today and stay in bed?"

Smiling, she ran her finger along his jaw. "We'll go and then tonight, as soon as Jessie Lou leaves, we'll have the house to ourselves. How does that sound?"

"Okay, but staying in bed and making love all day sounds better."

She laughed and stepped out of bed, taking the sheet with her. "I'm off to shower upstairs in my own bathroom."

"Do you realize I have never even seen that sanctuary of yours upstairs? You have never invited me up for so much as a peek."

She turned to reply to him, but her answer was momentarily forgotten. He had propped up the pillows and lay against them. A light blanket was pulled across his lap and his hands were behind his head as he looked at her.

Her mouth went dry and she wanted to go back and kiss him again, feel the reassurance of his strong arms around her. She worried that when she walked away, she was going to lose him again.

He sat up slightly and lowered his arms. "Maddie? You look upset. What is it, hon?"

She walked back to him, to sit on the side of the bed and kiss him. He wrapped his arms tightly around her, pulling her onto his lap as he kissed her. He was aroused again, ready to love. She kissed him passionately, slipping her arms around him, wanting to hold him against her heart.

She leaned away finally, pulling the sheet back up. His searching gaze went over her face while he combed her hair from her face with his fingers. "What is it?"

"I've found you again. I don't want to lose you a second time."

For a moment he frowned and then he smiled and hugged her. "You're not going to lose me. Not anytime soon." His voice lowered, took on a husky whisper. "If we stay in bed all day, you'll feel more reassured."

He was teasing, making light of the moment to cheer her or to allay her fears or to just put her off. She didn't know what he felt. She gathered the sheet, stood and turned. "I'll still go shower and start breakfast." At the door she turned back. He sat on the side of the bed, the blanket across his lap. It was obvious he was aroused. His hair was a tangle and he had a dark stubble of beard on his chin.

"And tonight you can come up and see my very private bedroom."

Smiling, she left the room and quickly climbed the stairs. The sooner they got going, the sooner they'd get home. She couldn't wait to share her bed with Jake.

As she dressed, she glanced out the window and saw Charley pause in front of the garage door. He glanced around. He had a gas can in his hand. He stepped inside the garage and closed the door quickly.

She wondered what he was doing. She yanked on her clothes and raced down the steps and out a side door, running to the garage.

She opened the door carefully, trying to avoid noise, and slid inside. The light was on and she could smell gasoline.

She tiptoed toward the truck she had been taking each day. Charley stood waiting while gas drained into the can he had been carrying.

"Charley, what are you doing?"

He whirled around and took a deep breath. "You have water in your gas tank. The last gas we got had water. I'm draining the vehicles."

She stared at him and shook her head. "You work for me now."

"I'm trying to take care of your truck. You'll use it today. I'll fill it with good gasoline."

She stared at him, hanging on to her temper. "My dad has hired you to cause trouble for me, hasn't he?"

Charley's lips clamped together and his face flushed.

"You work for me now. Make a choice. You either give me your loyalty or you get another job. You no longer work for my dad. You cut the tree, or had others cut it and place it on the bridge, didn't you?"

He stared at her without replying.

"You don't even have to answer. Pour my gas back into my truck unless you've put something in it. Which is it? Do you work for me or my dad?"

Silence stretched between them as he shifted from one foot to the other. "Your dad thinks Jake Calhoun is up to no good and using the search for a reason to get on Milan land. You know your father has your interests at heart."

"Charley, who are you going to work for?"

Another silence stretched between them. "Your father said I could come to work for him in town anytime," Charley finally replied. "He needs a handyman and caretaker and he said he can keep me busy. I'm getting older and some of the men don't like what I'm doing. I'll pack and go to work for your dad."

"Good enough. I'll have a check ready for you at the end of the day and you can get your things and leave when you're ready."

He nodded. "He always said this was in your best interests."

She didn't reply. "Have you done anything else to hamper our search?"

"No. I remember when you were born. We go back a long way. Your father's intentions are good."

"Get my truck ready to go," she said, trying to hang on to her temper because her real anger was with her dad.

She turned and left, hurrying back to the side door. She decided to say nothing to Jake until the search was over and Charley had gone. Jake might not be as kind.

After breakfast they left for another day of searching that turned out to be as fruitless as all the previous days of looking.

When they arrived back at her house, she glanced at Jake. "I heard from Wyatt today. He's stopping by and

Tony is with him. Do you care if I ask them to stay for dinner?"

"Of course not. I'll be glad to see Wyatt. I see him around town, but we just say hello and keep going. I don't know Tony as well, but we've met. Do they know I'm here?"

"Yes, they do."

"I know Tony does not like the Calhouns at all and I'll have to admit, my sister is pretty rotten right back at him."

Madison smiled. "I know. I told him no fights. Wyatt is always too closed up and in control to ever lose it and get in a fight. Besides, you and Wyatt played football together and you both did well with the other's help."

"That's for sure. He made me look good and vice versa."

"Maybe he wants to talk about the old football games you played. You two helped carry that team to some championships. The quarterback and the wide receiver. You were a good match."

"Wyatt was a fantastic receiver. He should have played pro longer than two years."

"He didn't like being away from his ranch. He could afford to turn down football so he did. And even though he probably will be glad to see you and reminisce about the glory days, I think he's coming by to check you out and see what you're up to on this hunt. They may want to see the map. Now that I think of it, I should have called them because they know the ranch better than I do."

"I'm guessing football might not be the only topic," Jake said with a harsh note. "Your dad probably wants *Sheriff* Milan to ask me a few questions."

"Maybe, but if Tony starts the questioning, it will be purely what Tony is wanting to know and nothing more. He's too involved in his ranch to care about gold or bones."

Jake smiled. "Gotta love the cowboys. I saw where Tony won a bareback bronc event recently."

"His office at his ranch is filled with his trophies and he has belt buckles galore."

"Tell them to come on. I'll be glad to see both of them. And I don't mind answering Wyatt's questions. Wyatt's a good guy."

"I think so. I like my brothers—most of the time."

Jake grinned. "The same with my siblings. Lindsay can be a brat, but she's growing up and she's turning into a damn good rancher. We're all scattered and now that our folks are retired and living in California, we don't get the family together as often as we used to."

"Us, too," Madison agreed. "And my brothers probably call me a brat, too. Although Tony can be the real brat. Wyatt was just born grown. He's always been responsible and levelheaded and the most take-charge one."

"Good to have one in every family."

"Spoken like the man who's the one in his family," she remarked with a grin.

He smiled back at her as they approached the rear of the house and saw her two brothers sitting on the porch. "Your brothers may have beaten us here, but I'm getting a shower."

"Amen to that one and I think they'll want us to shower."

"Yeah, it's been a hot, dirty, unsuccessful day."

"Maybe we can do something about that later," she teased.

"I'm holding you to that one," he said. "And getting to visit the inner sanctum on the second floor."

"Of course. I'll try to wear something special."

"Something really special would be maybe a handkerchief."

She laughed and he grinned. "You're laughing, but I mean it," he added.

As they approached her two brothers, she reminded

him, "Shower quickly and get in there to talk football. I'll let Jessie Lou know there will be four for dinner."

On the porch Tony had his tan hat pushed down above his eyes and was seated with his booted feet perched on the railing. Wyatt sat the same way, his brown hair showing from beneath his black Western hat. His badge was on his shirt while his firearm was out of sight, but she was certain it was on his hip.

Both of them remained seated until she and Jake reached the top step. Wyatt unfolded with a lazy motion and a slow grin, his six-foot-five-inch frame stretching over Tony, who was only an inch over six feet. Wyatt was the oldest and the tallest sibling. He grinned as he extended his hand to Jake.

"Good to see you again, Jake. You don't come to town often."

"No, I don't. It's good to see you."

Madison greeted her brothers as Jake shook hands with Tony.

"We have to clean up before we can socialize, so you two will just have to get a beer and find a comfortable spot to wait," Madison said as they walked through the back entryway. All three men removed their hats and hung them on a large hat rack inside the door.

"I take it you haven't found any buried treasure yet," Tony said, curiosity in his blue eyes that were flecked with green.

"No. Not a thing," she replied.

"I'll show you two the old map I have," Jake said. "You both know this land, probably as well as Madison."

"Better," she said. "There are extra copies of the map in the library."

"I've got mine right here," Jake said, fishing a copy from his hip pocket to hand it to Wyatt. "Look at that and see what you think."

"Will do," Wyatt answered. "But first things first. Let's find the fridge and get a beer. Then I'll look at your map. As kids, Tony and I spent plenty of time digging for that damn treasure."

"Have you had this map all these years?" Tony asked.

"Yep, my father and grandfather had it," Jake replied. "It's been passed down through generations. I suppose Madison told you I want to see if we can find where the gunfight was and have our ancestors' bones moved to the family cemetery and given a proper burial with a marker. No one thought about bringing the bones back until last Christmas when we got to talking about it and that's what brought this about. That and a deed. In our family, it's always been said there was a deed that gave some Mc-Cracken land to the Calhouns, over where the ranches border each other."

"That would be worth a search. Far more than any legend about a treasure, I'd think," Tony said.

"I agree," Jake replied. "I had some time on my hands and I figured I had put this off long enough." He nodded to her two brothers. "For now, though, I'm going to shower. We can talk about the map when I get done. Meanwhile, you guys go study it," Jake said as he headed for his suite.

"We'll be in the library," Wyatt replied.

Madison took her time to shower and change, expecting the three men to pore over the map and the aerial photos and discuss the best places to search. Maybe *argue* about the best places. All three were strong-willed, take-charge men.

Only one of those men dominated her thoughts right now. She couldn't stop thinking of Jake and the night that awaited them. As if a dam had broken, she was swamped by a running current of desire. Desire she no longer fought.

Beer in hand, Jake went to meet the two Milan brothers. As soon as he entered the library, he joined Wyatt and

Tony at the table with the pictures spread before them and a map on the computer.

Wyatt wasted no time with small talk. "There's one spot we agree on," he said, pointing to the map. "Then we each have places the other doesn't have. See this outcropping and this rock formation?"

Jake studied the drawing. "Yeah. Madison and I couldn't decide what that was—it doesn't exactly look like rocks. It almost looks as if they were trying to draw a steer—maybe to represent a herd of cattle."

"I don't think so," Wyatt said. "When I was ten years old I remember where they were going to build a line shack for ranch hands to have a place to stay out on the ranch. There was a rock formation that looked like a snowman. I was a kid and wanted to save it. Dad said that it would fall apart anyway, so I watched them blow it up, but I think I remember where it was."

"Come with us, Wyatt," Jake said. "Both of you if you want," he added, glancing at Tony.

"I can't this week. I have some appointments and need to be in Lubbock for a court case that involves several counties," Wyatt replied.

"I can't, either. Maybe later if you don't have success," Tony added. "Look, I think this resembles your map," he said, pointing to another place on the map on the computer and placing the map on the photo.

"I hope you've found better places than I did." At the sound of Madison's voice Jake turned to see her walk into the room.

When he did, he forgot the map and the treasure. All he could focus on was Madison in cutoffs. Her long legs were fabulous, muscled enough to be shapely, lean enough to be sexy. He remembered them wrapped around him last night.

He wanted to untie the scarf that held her hair and peel away her blouse.

As much as he wanted to hear Tony's and Wyatt's thoughts, he hoped they ended their visit quickly and left him alone with Madison.

It was an effort to turn his attention back to the map and he tried to listen to Tony, who was talking and pointing. Madison came to stand beside him, moving into a space between Wyatt and him.

Jake could detect the scent of her perfume, reminding him of moments last night when they had made love and he caught whiffs of her perfume.

He couldn't resist just a glance at her. Once again his mind betrayed him and he was flooded with memories of last night, her warm, soft body in his arms, her luscious curves that took his breath. Would old feelings rekindle now that they both knew what had happened and who was really to blame?

"What do you think, Jake?" she said, turning to look up at him.

The only thoughts he had were on making love to her. He tried to pick up the conversation because all three Milans stared at him.

"Your brothers have some new ideas about this. They think Rocky Creek cut an entirely different path, farther to the west," he said, hoping that wasn't a repetition of whatever had just been said.

Jake leaned over the photos, and pointed out places to Madison that Wyatt and Tony had picked.

"Some of these aren't anywhere near the creek," Madison said. "I think the map looks as if there is a creek running through it."

"I don't think this line is Rocky Creek. I don't think it's a creek at all, or if it is, it dried up years ago," Wyatt said.

"It looks like a creek," Madison said, leaning closer.

"I agree with Madison," Tony said. "But I also agree with Wyatt that it may have dried up before 1900."

"We'll hunt in different places tomorrow—away from Rocky Creek—and see what we can find," Jake said.

Madison stepped back. "While y'all hash over the possibilities, I'll see if Jessie Lou needs help with dinner."

"Good idea," Tony said, patting his flat stomach.

"Tony, you eat like a nineteen-year-old. Constantly," she added and he grinned, flashing straight white teeth. "I'll let you know when it's ready," she said and left the room.

After dinner everyone thanked Jessie Lou. She stayed in the kitchen to clean while Madison and the men returned to the library, once again studying pictures and the copies of the map. Jake thought it was a good idea because he wanted to go over the map carefully with each of them.

"Look. I haven't attributed any significance to these small circles," Wyatt said. "I figured it was rocks or just circles. They don't look like something that would indicate buried treasure. At first, I didn't even notice them and then I thought they looked like doodling, maybe to throw someone off, but they could have some purpose."

All three Milans bent over the map on the table and Jake's gaze ran over Madison's back and down over her bottom. He wanted to reach out and touch her. He longed to untie the scarf that held her hair behind her head and let her hair fall free around her face.

Jake picked up the copy of the map and looked at it. "Tough part will be finding where this is as well as whatever it is. If that isn't Rocky Creek, all we can do is look to see what else you think the circles might depict."

"Try the places we've suggested," Wyatt said.

"Frankly, I think the buried treasure is just a crazy myth," Tony said. "I'll be shocked if you find anything."

"You may be right," Jake replied, "but I've thought about this off and on the past couple of years. Right now I have some time when I can get away, so I'm glad the Milans are letting a Calhoun onto their land," he said, smiling at Madison, who smiled in return.

"Let us know how it comes out," Wyatt said, heading for the back door.

Madison and Jake followed. Wyatt and Tony each put on his hat and on the porch, Jake shook hands with first one and then the other.

"Thanks again for not objecting to my search."

"You're agreeing to give us the treasure if you find it and we'll get our ancestors' bones, too. Sounds like a good deal to me," Wyatt said, his blue eyes searching Jake's.

"Right. I hope to find the deed that gives us some Mc-Cracken land. He won't miss it. He has a big ranch."

"Well, I better get on home," Wyatt said.

"I have to go, too," Tony said. "I'm going out tonight."

As the brothers went down the porch steps, Jake and Madison stood at the top step watching them go. Jake wanted to drape his arm around her, but he fought the impulse.

As soon as they stepped inside, he reached behind him to close the door and lock it and then he turned to face her. She had walked away a few steps.

"Madison, come here," he said in a deep voice.

She turned and he didn't wait for her. He closed the distance between them and took her into his arms.

Eight

Madison's heart skipped a beat and she drew a deep breath. She was in Jake's arms—where she'd fantasized about being all night. More than anything she wanted his kisses. Right now. She gave no thought to the future, to a relationship with him; she thought only of this moment. She felt desire and a need to wipe out the years of bad feelings between them. "I want to forget," she said, looking up at him. "I want our loving to destroy the bad memories, the anger and hurt for both of us."

"Yes," he agreed. "In some ways, it's as if we just met and in some ways, it's as if I've known you forever."

Before she could answer, he leaned closer and his mouth covered hers, making her forget conversation.

She tightened her arms around his waist, holding him close, kissing him passionately in return, her heartbeat racing. Desire swept through her as she ran her hands over his back and then tugged his shirt out of his jeans.

Clothing was an unwanted barrier. While he continued

to kiss her, he picked her up and carried her to his bedroom, where he stood her on her feet.

"Jake," she whispered, stepping back to unbuckle his belt, wanting to make love while at the same time wanting to prolong the kisses and caresses for hours. It was Jake she was making love to and that seemed the best thing possible and so incredibly right.

They made love all through the night and when she woke right before dawn, she found herself lying against him, their legs entangled, her head in the hollow of his shoulder, her hair spread over his shoulder, arm and chest. Jake held her with one arm and combed long strands of her hair from her face. Rising on his elbow, he tucked her against him and smiled down at her while he continued to comb her hair from her face in slow, feathery strokes that made her tingle.

"You are so beautiful, Maddie."

"Thank you." She smiled sleepily. "You're the only person who has ever called me Maddie. I like it."

"Good. You were right, what you said. Making love to you does help soften the past. It's a rediscovery of you, but we're both different people now. You can never get back the past."

"I know you can't," she said. "We can't go back and pick up from where we were."

He shook his head. "No. We can start from here and see where we go, and so far, it's good."

They were both quiet, her thoughts in turmoil over the revelations and changes, the emotional upheavals again in her life. What did she feel for Jake now? Would she ever rekindle the feelings she'd had for him?

She couldn't answer her own questions. There had been so much hurt and anger between them; once that was gone, what did they have? In some ways she barely knew him. Their lives had gone separate ways.

She sat up and pulled a sheet beneath her arms, turning to look down at him.

"I've decided we'll talk to you about leasing land on my ranch."

For a moment he was silent while his eyes narrowed. "All right. I'll let someone know. We'll set up an appointment with you."

He pulled her down again beside him. They were both silent and she suspected the moment had changed for him as much as it had for her.

"Thanks for the change of heart."

"Now that I know the truth, why wouldn't I talk to you about leasing our land? Our lives have had another monumental change."

He drew her close to hold her and they were both quiet. Finally she moved away and again pulled the sheet under her arms. Holding it close, she stepped out of bed. "Today is Sunday and I'll go to church. You and the guys can search. I don't care. I told Stoney and Darren to go to church if they want."

"I'll go home and regroup, then. That's what my guys did last night."

Smiling, she walked out of the room, aware of his gaze still on her and the questions still in her mind. She didn't know the answers. All she knew was she didn't want to lose him a second time.

Upstairs, she gathered fresh clothes and went to shower, moving routinely, her thoughts still wrapped up in Jake and the changes that had transpired. Already, she wanted to get back with him and she wanted more of his kisses and lovemaking.

Jake showered, shaved and pulled on fresh clothes. All the time he dressed he thought about Madison and her willingness to talk to his company about leasing Milan land.

He sent a text to Lindsay and to his brothers to tell them about the change in events. He also explained that he had told Madison the truth and she had flown to Dallas to confront her father and the judge had verified it.

Lindsay answered promptly with a brief text: Hooray!

He got a congratulatory one from Josh, while Mike urged him to get a lease signed soon.

He glanced out the window, but instead of seeing the land spreading away from the house, he saw her green eyes and lush body. What did he really feel for her?

He couldn't answer his own question. Lust was paramount now. Already he wanted to make love to her again. He couldn't get enough of her, and her appetite for lovemaking seemed as insatiable as his, which made him desire her even more.

He combed his hair and went to find her.

On Monday they spent another day searching and finding nothing except dirt, roots and rocks. At the house, Jessie Lou had the night off, and Jake had agreed to grill steaks.

Madison turned when she heard Jake enter the kitchen and her heart missed a beat. His black shirt emphasized his muscles and his dark eyes and hair, his broad shoulders. She thought about their lovemaking and fought the urge to go kiss him.

"Want a drink?" she asked instead.

"I'll get a beer. I'll pour wine for you."

"Just a small glass, thanks. I have the steaks ready for you to grill." They got drinks and he carried the steaks outside. While they waited for the grill to get hot, they sat with their drinks.

"Whenever you want, we can set a time to discuss leasing land."

She was surprised. "Don't you need to look it over first?"

He shook his head. "We're far more familiar with this ranch than you'd guess. Several ranches around here, in fact. Geologists have studied this area off and on through the past three years. This isn't the only likely spot, but it's a choice one."

"My, oh, my. I knew nothing about that."

He smiled. "Enough about business. You look great," he said, pulling his chair close to hers and holding her hand. "I want to take you out soon. Some night when we haven't spent a day digging and searching for treasure."

"Name the time." She grinned as she said, "We'll start all sorts of rumors the first time we're seen together. Has word gotten back to your parents in California?"

"Not yet, but I imagine it will by tomorrow from Lindsay."

"Lindsay," Madison repeated his sister's name. "I'll bet she's not one bit happy. Lindsay does not like the Milans and I'll have to admit that Tony probably makes things worse."

"That he does. I know that for a fact. Don't pay any attention. She'll be friendly if I am." He paused to raise her hand and brush a feathery kiss on her palm. His breath was warm, his kiss making her tingle. She drew a deep breath and wanted to be in his arms. He looked up into her eyes while he continued to hold her hand.

"You're definitely hungry?" he asked in a raspy voice.

"I'm famished," she whispered, looking at his mouth. He wanted to make love. His dark eyes conveyed his desire and she responded. Her body grew warmer, and she wanted to step over and sit in his lap. "Jake, we should eat," she whispered.

"Come here, Maddie," he said, taking her drink from her other hand to set it on a table. His fingers tightened around her hand and he tugged lightly. She stood and he pulled her closer, down to his lap, where he wrapped his arms around her and kissed her.

In minutes she pushed against his chest and sat back. "Jake, we're not wasting dinner." She could barely say the words. She stood and walked away from him.

He followed and stepped to the grill to put the steaks on.

"I'll get the rest of the dinner on the table," she said, going inside. She inhaled deeply, trying to cool herself, to get through dinner before it got burned or wasted, but she couldn't stop thinking about afterward and making love the rest of the night. Once again those nagging questions bombarded her, questions about a potential relationship with Jake, about a future. She banished them from her mind and glanced outside to see him standing in front of the grill while a dark cloud of smoke rose and dissipated into the air. Jake was incredibly handsome. It was difficult to think about dinner when all she wanted was to go back to bed.

The steaks were thick, juicy, delicious, but after a few bites her appetite vanished.

"You'll go back to Dallas soon, won't you?" she asked him. "I've been told you're rarely at the ranch."

"That's right. I'd like to be here, but I'm too busy. I've blocked out this week and next week. How long are you here on the ranch before you'll go to New Mexico?"

"I go after Christmas to New Mexico and come back here in late spring for about a month."

"Any chance you'll stay in Dallas some of that time?"

"Maybe," she said, smiling at him.

"I want to see you after this search is over."

"I'd like that," she replied. They gazed in silence at each other. She could see desire in his dark eyes while all she wanted was to be in his arms.

"I don't think you're any hungrier than I am," he said.

"I seem to remember that I was promised a visit to your suite upstairs, but that's never happened."

She stood and he came to his feet at the same time. "That's because we never get that far when heading to a bedroom. C'mon. I'll show you around my digs."

Smiling, he joined her, draping his arm across her shoulders and pulling her close against him. She was aware of his height, his warmth. She tingled with anticipation and fought the urge to stop to kiss him now.

"When I'm in Dallas or farther away and I call you, I want to be able to envision you in your room. Right now that's a blank."

"So you're going to call me?"

"Yes, I am," he said, turning her to face him as they stopped at the foot of the stairs. "I want to see where this is going." His gaze roamed over her features. "We're not the same people we were and we have a lot that has happened between us."

"In some ways we hardly know each other at all."

"That's right, but what I know, I like," he said, his voice getting husky and her heartbeat quickening while her gaze went to his mouth.

"That tour upstairs is going to have to wait a little longer," he whispered before he leaned down to kiss away her reply.

Over an hour later they were still in the bed in his suite. They were lying facing each other and she loved the feel of him toying with long strands of her hair.

"You know, Maddie, I haven't even seen your artwork except the few pictures you showed me downstairs. You're a famous, successful artist but I've always ignored your publicity. You must have other artwork here. You must have a studio somewhere in this house, too. By the way, I haven't seen the whole house, either."

"I think it's your fault that we have limited our seeing the house to the kitchen, the family room, library and your bedroom."

He grinned, flashing snow-white, even teeth. Locks of his dark hair fell over his forehead. "I want to see your bedroom and your studio."

"Then I suggest we get dressed and you keep your hands to yourself and I will try to do the same."

"Keep your hands to myself?" he said.

"You know what I meant." Aware of his steady gaze, she stepped out of bed and began to pick up her clothing. "I will go up and shower and you come up when you're ready."

"Or we could save time and shower here and both go up together."

"I don't really think that would be a time-saver at all. See you upstairs," she said as she left the room.

She showered, dressed in cutoffs and pulled on a bright pink T-shirt. As she brushed her hair, she heard a light knock.

"Anybody home?" Jake stood in the doorway. He was barefoot, wearing jeans and shirtless.

"Oh, honey," she said, crossing the sitting area to him to wrap one arm around his waist and run her hand over his muscled chest. "I would never keep a handsome man like you out," she drawled in a sultry rasp.

He grinned and started to lean down to kiss her. She moved back. "I'll give you the tour first," she said, taking his hand and walking into the hall. She released his hand to wave her fingers. "To the east is the wing with three bedrooms and one smaller bedroom suite. Here in the center of the house…" She glanced at him and momentarily lost her train of thought. Jake had stepped back, leaning one shoulder against the wall with his feet crossed and a hand on his hip while his gaze roamed slowly over her legs.

She tingled and forgot the tour. Her mouth went dry and the temperature around her spiked. "Jake, you're not paying attention," she whispered.

"Oh, I'm paying real close attention. Those are the best-looking legs in Texas and that is saying a lot."

"Thank you, but I believe you're ready for glasses. I can't live up to that description," she said, crossing the distance to him. "Do you want the tour or not?"

He looked down at her, his gaze going to her mouth, and her heart skipped a beat. She tightened her arm around his waist, turning her face up slightly.

"Yeah, give me the tour," he replied and his voice was as raspy as her own.

Surprised, because his words did not match his actions, she waved her hand in a semicircle. "Here in the center are two large bedroom suites. One was my parents' all the years we were growing up and they still stay there if they come to visit me." She moved on to another bedroom suite. "I have taken this one because it's so large and more convenient than being in one of the wings. Now to the west wing," she said, facing west. "There are four more middle-size bedroom suites. One was mine growing up, one was Wyatt's, one was Nick's and one was Tony's. Although Nick rarely sees his ranch, they all have their own ranches now and my dad deeded this one to me. Nick prefers Dallas and Austin. I think he keeps his ranch for an investment."

"You said they gave you the ranch three years ago?"

"Yes, after they started living in Dallas so much. I was out of school and beginning to do well with my painting and Dad said he was giving me the ranch partially because of the success I had made of my art. He helped the others buy their ranches."

"Did it ever occur to you that he might have been so generous to make up for what he did when you were going to elope?"

Startled, she stared at Jake as she shook her head. "No. No, I don't think so."

Jake looked around, dropping the subject.

"Down this hall past the bedrooms is a large room I've had converted into a studio," she said, leading him into a room that had tables, two oversize sinks, easels, racks with brushes and tubes of paint. Canvases, some finished, some in various stages from pencil sketches, were on easels, propped on the floor and hanging on the walls.

He walked over to look at them. "You're really very talented," he said. "I'm impressed."

"I'm glad," she said, smiling at him. "Now, back to my suite." She took his hand and they entered her suite, where she paused to look around.

She glanced at the familiar surroundings of the sitting room, the red, white and green decor, the antique mahogany furniture, the polished plank floor with a thick red area rug in the center. He followed her to an adjoining room, where she held out her hand, waving toward the bedroom.

She walked inside with him, where the same red, white and green decor was used. A four-poster mahogany queen-size bed stood in the center of the room. As she turned to say something to him, the words never came. Looking at her mouth, Jake stepped close to slip his arms around her.

As his lips covered hers, her heart thudded. She wrapped her arms around his neck and held him tightly, wanting his kisses as if it were the first time he had kissed her. She wanted to make love, to hold and kiss him. Even more, she wanted to get to know him again.

They made love long into the night.

By then she had decided she would lease the ranchland to him. She suspected it would be a very good deal for her and would top the other offers they had had.

Other decisions weren't so easily made. Would they fall in love again? Had she already and didn't realize this was the real thing? She was uncertain, something that thirteen years ago she wouldn't have thought possible. She had been so wildly in love with him then. Now she was scared to let go and she didn't know what he felt.

As she ran her fingers lightly over his chest, she kept telling herself one thing: time would tell.

On Tuesday Madison returned to the search with the men. She took a sketch pad and drew while the men dug, pacing off a grid that she and Jake had planned and drawn.

Following her brothers' suggestions, they had moved away from the creek and were in an arroyo that was dry. They worked in the sun and even though it was a fall day, the temperature was in the nineties and Jake's shirt was plastered to his body. She still wanted to come along, in case they found something, but now that she trusted Jake and had no worry about him deceiving her, she decided this would be the last day she would go with them.

When they broke for lunch they went back to where they had parked the trucks in a grove of acacias along the creek to keep the vehicles in the shade.

She sat eating a sandwich with Jake. He had brought a fresh cotton shirt and pulled it on. It was unbuttoned, the shirttail hanging out over his jeans.

He hadn't shaved this morning and had dark stubble on his jaw. His hair was in a tangle with ends wet from his sweat. In spite of the dust, sweat and stubble, he looked sexy and appealing and she thought about the evening, looking forward with anticipation.

"I need to go home and get some other boots tonight. I forgot to bring them this morning. Come home with me and we'll eat there. You've never been in my house."

"All right. Are we coming back to mine or staying at yours?"

"Stay at mine tonight, Maddie," he said, his gaze stirring a sizzling current, making her wish the afternoon would not be so long.

"You have a deal, but I'll need some clothes. What about stopping at the house when we go back and letting me pick up a few things?"

He nodded. "Sure. You're the first woman to stay there, you know."

"That surprises me. You were so eager to marry. I'm surprised you haven't had a serious relationship, let alone that you're still single."

"I've been busy and there never has been anyone I've been that serious about. And I got burned badly, so I've skirted around serious romantic entanglements."

"I married out of spite."

"I always wondered if you were as in love with him as we had been," Jake said quietly.

"Not ever. It was a dreadful mistake that I knew I was making and I got out of it early on because it was messing up Will's life."

"Damn," Jake said quietly, setting down his half-eaten sandwich. "I hope you told your dad."

"I did and he looked pained and said he was afraid of that. It's over and done and I'm sorry if I hurt Will. I wasn't thinking clearly and I was so angry with you at the time."

She met Jake's level gaze. "I hate that," he said and she shrugged.

"As you would say, it's over. Forget it."

His gaze shifted beyond her while he seemed lost in his thoughts for a moment. "That's true," he said and picked up his bottle of water to take a long drink. He waved the bottle at her. "This is the best part of lunch."

"It'll be hotter this afternoon."

"We can swim when we get to my house."

"Sure," she said, smiling at him. He had been about to

take a bite of sandwich, but he lowered it and looked at her with raised eyebrows.

"You have something else in mind when we arrive at my house?"

"You don't?"

He grinned. "I wish we were alone now."

"I promise you, it would not do you any good out here with the ground full of cactus pines, cockleburs and snakes possibly crawling past. Not ever."

"There's a challenge if I ever heard one."

She pointed a finger at him. "Well, we're not alone, so forget it. Eat your sandwich and look forward to finishing here for today."

"Oh, I am looking forward to it," he said in a husky, seductive drawl while his gaze roamed slowly from her head to her toes, making her tingle in its wake. "It's going to be difficult to concentrate on digging holes in the ground this afternoon. My thoughts will be elsewhere."

"It doesn't take great powers of concentration to dig," she said, smiling at him. When he gave her a sexy grin, she began to count down the hours.

In the hot afternoon sun, Jake dug, thinking the treasure could be buried at her ranch house for all they knew. He paused, leaning on his shovel while he glanced at Maddie, who sat with her head bent over her drawing pad while she sketched. Where were they going with their relationship?

She didn't seem to have an answer any more than he did. Sex was hot, the best, and he couldn't get enough of her, but did it go deeper than that? Was he so blinded by desire that he couldn't even perceive the depth of his feelings for her? Did he care if they walked out of each other's lives when this search was over?

He cared about that. In fact, he wanted her to move in with him, but it was a purely lustful longing. He didn't feel the way he had at nineteen—as if she was necessary for his life to continue. At that age he couldn't imagine life without her. They were teenagers and both wildly in love in the way that only teens could be. It had been intense, dramatic and youthful, a love that had been totally entwined with hot sex that she experienced for the first time in her life.

Her father had turned his world upside down. Jake still didn't like to think about how badly it had hurt to lose her.

What about now? He needed to get a reading on what he felt for her, because she would walk out of his life again soon and there might not ever be another chance. Was it going to hurt to tell her goodbye?

With the hot sun beating down on his shoulders and back, he stood looking at her. The thought of her going her own way made his stomach churn. Their time together was coming to an end and he didn't want it to—but was that love or just lust?

From what she had said to him, she was as uncertain as he was about the extent of her feelings. He envied the certainty he had felt at nineteen, never questioning if he truly loved her enough to want to spend the rest of his life with her. He had been so sure and it had taken a lot of pain, time and anger to kill those feelings.

Common sense said to step away, get the physical relationship in perspective and see how he felt. That was common sense, but it didn't appeal to him.

He fished out his phone to call his ranch to tell his cook to put out two steaks for him to grill, and to fix the rest of the dinner and put it in the refrigerator for tonight. He returned to digging, thinking about Maddie and their lovemaking last night and looking forward to tonight. There had never been any woman in his life he had felt so strongly about as he had Maddie. That made him search his feelings now more than ever. If they really fell in love, surely they would each recognize it.

As he dug it dawned on him that if they found the deed, he would have a dilemma—all the more reason to decide soon what his feelings were for her. Now that she would let him lease her land to drill, the whole reason for searching for the deed had vanished.

He didn't want to hurt her. That was one certainty in his life. For Maddie's sake, he would never take any of the Milan land. When he'd thought it would affect her dad, he'd wanted to take it and enjoy every minute when he could tell Judge Milan that part of his ranch now belonged to the Calhouns. That would be sweet revenge. But the ranch was now owned by Maddie. Taking part of it would hurt her, so he wasn't going to do it. He didn't really think the deed existed anyway. With the lack of success they had been having, he figured the old legend was just a tall Texas tale and nothing more.

He couldn't wait to get to the ranch, clean up and enjoy the evening with Maddie.

By Wednesday, Jake's hopes had plummeted. Monday he would be in Dallas, back in the corporate life. When would he see Maddie once he was in Dallas or traveling and she was out here at the ranch?

He loved being a rancher, loved everything about the cowboy life and living on the ranch. The quiet was something he occasionally had to come home and enjoy. But he had only days left.

He plunged the shovel into the hard earth and tossed a shovelful of dirt to one side. "Your ranch looks as if an army of gophers have taken over," he said to Madison, who sat on a nearby rock and sketched.

Once again they were near Rocky Creek. They were in the shade of another grove of trees, digging in ground slightly less packed, and she had found a rock where she could sit and draw.

"What do you say to us stopping at four today? If we haven't found anything by then, I'm giving up for today. We have tomorrow to try one more time. Tomorrow I'll pay the guys a bonus for helping this week—yours and mine."

"You don't have to do that. I can pay the ones who work for me."

He shook his head. "No, this has been my project from the start. It's like chasing rainbows. I insist."

She shrugged. "Okay. Thanks. That's nice." His gaze raked over her. She was dressed to be out on the ranch—boots, jeans, long-sleeved cotton shirt and a broad-brimmed tan Stetson that looked as if she had had it since high school.

"Back to quitting at four. Let's go home, get dressed and let me take you to Dallas tonight to dinner, maybe dancing. I have a home in Dallas and we can just stay in the city. We've earned a night out. Will you go with me?"

A big smile broke out on her face that made his heart-beat quicken. She was irresistible to him when she smiled. "You have a deal," she said.

"Great. Think you can be ready to go by six?"

"Oh, yes. Easily."

"Half past five?" he asked and she thought a moment before she nodded.

"That's it, then," he said. "If I can get home, shower and get back. If not, I won't be much later than that, but I'm definitely aiming for half past five."

"I can't wait. I haven't been out to dinner and dancing with an exciting, handsome man in way too long."

"I hope not since you were sixteen."

She laughed and his grin widened.

"It was a little later than that, but it was not in the past few months."

"Not what I wanted to hear."

"Forget it. I'm going with you tonight."

"So you are and I can't wait." He wanted to chuck this whole search and head home now, but this was next to the last day he could devote to this, so he would stay until four. He jammed the shovel into the ground to get another scoop of dirt and scraped something hard.

Nine

Madison heard the metallic click of Jake's shovel striking something and looked around. She stood up from the rock and walked closer to watch, her eyes meeting Jake's.

"Keep your fingers crossed."

Jake turned to call two of the closest men. "Stoney, Russ, can you come here?"

Both of them came with shovels in hand.

"I've hit something. Help dig here so we can get to it quicker."

They joined him, digging, and Russ struck something after the third shovelful of dirt.

She stood in silence watching them uncover what looked like a piece of battered and scratched black metal. In minutes they began to enlarge the hole. The more dirt they removed the better she could see a large metal box with handles on each side and a smaller handle in the center of the top. Excitement gripped her along with curiosity, far more to see if the legend was actually true than to expect any real treasure.

Soon dirt was dug away from the box and Jake leaned down to pick it up. The other two men bent over to help. Her excitement mounted when it was obvious that the box was heavy. Because it was below them in the ground, it was awkward to grasp, and required all their strength to lift it out unless they dug a larger hole.

Jake called over his shoulder and the other men came to see as Jake and Russ set the box on the ground. She noticed a keyhole on the front of the box. When Jake tried to open it, the lid didn't move.

"It's locked," he said, looking around for a rock. "We're not digging for a key," he remarked. Someone handed him a rock and Jake grasped it to swing hard. After the third hit, the lid budged a fraction. Jake opened it and sunlight glinted on gold coins.

The men broke out in applause.

Madison could barely believe her eyes. "You found it!" she exclaimed.

"That legend was true," Jake said. She could see the surprise on his face and she knew how he was feeling. He'd heard it all his life and had searched for it many times on the Calhoun ranch before trying the Milan ranch.

He picked up a coin and turned it in his hand, standing to show it to Madison while they both peered at it.

"It's from 1849. One side is a Liberty head, and the other is an eagle," Jake said, reading and turning the coin. It's a five-dollar gold coin. I'll be damned," he said, still turning the gold coin in his hand.

"Since you said the treasure is mine," Madison said, "I think everyone here should have ten coins." The men grinned and cheered and told her thanks.

"And you'll still get your bonus," Jake added.

Madison picked up a handful of coins to pass them out. "I'll have this appraised and find out what these are worth."

"I'm keeping mine," Stoney said. "Eighteen forty-nine was a long time ago."

Others agreed as they looked over the coins, turning the gold in their hands.

"This means the remains of our ancestors may be buried in this vicinity," Jake said, looking around. "I'll drive the truck up here and we'll lock this up in the truck. I don't know anything about old coins, but these are in good shape. I have a feeling they're worth a fortune—as long as they're real, and I think they are."

Jake gave orders about where to dig to search for the bones. As the men dispersed, he walked to Madison. "I'll go get the truck and one of them can help me load the box." He shook his head. "I'm still in shock that the legend is true."

"Jake, when we get that back to the house, I want you to take half the treasure. We don't know who that chest really belonged to, and some members of your family may want to keep the coins just because of the historical value. Those coins are part of the Old West, part of early-day Texas and part of our families' histories."

"I think you better reconsider your generous offer. Your brothers may not be happy if you give half away. I get along with Tony, but he doesn't like Calhouns."

"Tony doesn't begin to compare to Lindsay's dislike of Milans," she added. "The family feud lives on in those two."

"Our folks, also. And grandparents even more."

"I don't care who agrees and disagrees."

"That's generous, Maddie," he said. "But if you want to wait to talk to your family—"

"I'll talk them into accepting it," she said. She looked

around the site. "I hope we find the remains and I know you want the deed."

"Yeah. See you in a few minutes." She watched him stride away, his long legs covering the distance until he climbed into his pickup and drove toward her with the truck bouncing over the rough ground.

She couldn't stop her thoughts from returning to a few moments ago. When he'd opened the box, her first reaction was surprise that the legend was true. The thought that immediately followed was a sinking realization that Jake might possibly walk out of her life. Again.

Everything inside her felt squeezed and hurt. The reason for his presence in her life had ended. But she wasn't ready to say goodbye.

Over an hour later, Darren called out to Jake, "Mr. Calhoun, come look. I think I may have found some bones."

Madison had heard Jake instruct the men that they were not to disturb any bones they uncovered, but to wait and let the medical examiner tell them what to do. To her relief, that was what Darren was doing. While Darren stood leaning on his shovel, she hurried to catch up with Jake to go down to the creek bank.

"I hope we can tell whether these are human bones or animal bones," Jake said. "This is a grim discovery, but if it's our ancestors' remains it will be good to get them buried in a proper place."

She stood beside Jake and looked at a large bone. "I don't know much about bones, so I don't know whether it's from a human or not."

"Well, we'll find out from someone official," Jake said, then he turned to Darren. "Just keep looking carefully and see if you can find some more bones here."

She walked away from them, going back to get her sketch pad, but she couldn't take her eyes off Jake. He was strong and fit, sexy. She wanted to hold him and kiss him and she wanted them to make love far more than flying to Dallas for dinner and dancing. She wondered if she could get him to change the plans.

Now they had found the gold and the bones. Her time with Jake was over. She would go back to her artwork and he would return to Dallas and his energy business that probably caused him to travel often.

She didn't want to say goodbye to him. The mere thought of not seeing him hurt deep in her soul. The more time she spent with him, the more she wanted to be with him and the more she wanted him in her life. Permanently in her life. She had no idea how Jake felt and she wasn't going to tell him because he might not feel as strongly.

She was in love with him. It went beyond the love-making, beyond carnal desire. She loved him. Maybe she always had and there was never anyone else and never would be.

What if Jake didn't feel that way and walked out?

She couldn't answer her question, and she hoped she'd never have to.

Later, as they drove to Jake's ranch after having stopped at her house so she could pick up her things, she turned to face him. She placed her fingers lightly on his warm thigh. Instantly, his hand covered hers. "Jake, it's getting late. Let's just go to your ranch tonight instead of Dallas."

"Really? I don't want you to be disappointed if you had your heart set on Dallas, but truthfully, I'm glad to hear you say you'd rather stay here."

"It'll be a lot better. Frankly, I want to open the box and look at the gold. Besides, I can think of more fun ways to spend the evening than going to Dallas."

He glanced at her and then turned his attention to the highway. "When we're home, I'll show you what I've been thinking about all day long."

"You've been thinking about those gold coins," she said, smiling at him.

"Not nearly as much as making love to you," he said in a husky voice. "Just shower while I shower, wrap in a towel and I'll be ready and waiting."

"I figured we'd eat dinner, look at the coins and let our families know and *then* we would spend the rest of the evening in the best way possible," she said softly, stroking his thigh.

He covered her fingers again and held her hand against his leg. "Save the caresses for when we're home. I might wreck the truck."

She laughed softly and started to move her hand away, but his fingers tightened, holding her hand on his leg.

"When we get home, I'll take the box inside. Later tonight, much later, we can count the coins, but I agree we should let our families know. This is a big deal for us. That old legend was the truth—I'm still shocked. Deep down, I really didn't think we would ever find anything. Now we'll have to try to identify whose remains we have. We may not know all of our earliest ancestors who came to Texas."

"I know some of mine, but I don't know how they can specify which ones they might be."

"They should be able to decide which are Milans and which are Calhouns from our DNA, I'd think. I'll call tomorrow and see what to do with the remains."

She turned herself in her seat so she could face him. "This has been a most amazing day. Wyatt will probably want to come by tomorrow and see the coins."

"My whole family will come see them so we're telling them too late tonight for anyone to come to the ranch. I want you to myself with no interruptions."

"I'll get my brothers to come get the coins and take them to the bank. I'm sure word will travel about them and we need to get them secured tomorrow."

"I can do it for you if you'd like."

"Thanks, but I promise you, my brothers will be happy to take mine for me." She couldn't contain the grin that overtook her. "This is so exciting. It isn't the money as much as the link with the past."

"It's a link, but those coins may be worth a lot. It may surprise you."

She realized that an awful lot was surprising her these days.

She turned to look out the window then as they neared Jake's ranch. She glanced out at mesquite and cactus, an occasional acacia or a tall cottonwood. When they reached the entrance to his ranch, the gates were open. He drove across the cattle guard and headed down a graveled road.

Happiness filled her because she was with him and they would soon be alone for the evening. She studied his handsome profile, his straight nose and firm jaw, his prominent cheekbones. Always by the end of the day his black, wavy hair was in a tangle and stubble was beginning to show on his jaw.

She wanted to unbuckle her seat belt, scoot close to him and put her hands on him, but she controlled the impulse. They were almost to his ranch house. Soon she would be able to do what she wanted with him.

The road was winding and seemed long, but finally he drove to the back, parked and handed her a ring with keys. "You unlock the door and I'll give you the alarm code so you can switch it off. I'll carry the gold. It'll help if you'll hold the door."

"Sure you don't want me to help you?"

"No. I got it."

He climbed out and picked up the metal box. She closed the door and rushed ahead to get the back door unlocked. The alarm beeped as she held the door for him and he hurried past her. She punched in the code before the alarm went off, then locked the back door and turned to go look for Jake.

His home was far more ranch style than her parents' elegant house, and it looked comfortable and inviting. She found him in a spacious family room with a beamed ceiling and brown leather furniture. He had set the box on the floor, removed the lid and stood looking at the gold coins. All she could think was that it meant she would see the last of him.

He turned as she walked up. Slipping his arm around her, he pulled her close against his side. "Finding this was like finding a needle in a haystack. It's thanks to your brothers. That location was Wyatt's suggestion."

"It's great, Jake. I'm thrilled."

He looked down at her, tilting her face up to his. "I'd say let's shower together, but I'm really grubby. C'mon. I'll give you a room and we can get cleaned up. I meant it when I said you don't have to wear anything except a towel. That would suit me just fine. That would be even better than that box of gold coins."

Smiling at him, she wanted to pull his head down and kiss him, whether they had cleaned up or not. Her smile faded because desire made her heart pound. She gazed intently into his thickly lashed brown eyes and then she looked at his mouth.

His expression changed. Stepping closer, he slipped his arm around her waist to draw her close against him. "I'm dusty and sweaty."

"I don't care," she said, thinking he was appealing and sexy. With a moan, wanting him with all her being, she wrapped her arms around him and kissed him passionately. She poured her feelings into her kiss, all her longing, all her love for him that had returned full force if it had ever really gone at all.

His hand unfastened her buttons and yanked off her shirt. He had already tossed his aside.

With shaking fingers she undid his belt and jeans. Clothes and boots were tossed away. She could think only of Jake, wanting him desperately, feeling as if she might lose him again. He released her a moment to get protection and then he pulled her into his arms again.

While he kissed her, he picked her up and she wrapped her legs around him. Holding her tightly, he let her slide down so he could enter her, fill her. She was wrapped around him, kissing him as if it were her last time with him.

He thrust deep and fast, pumping his hips. Tension built, a physical need that swept her. He groaned while he kissed her, the sound muffled deep in his throat.

She cried out with her climax. "Jake!" she gasped. "I love you." She whispered the words, meaning them with all her heart, mindlessly lost in the moment as ecstasy and relief poured over her.

He slowed while she draped herself on him. "Jake," she whispered. She showered kisses on his face and throat, not caring about the salty taste of him. She held him tightly with her growing fear that when she let go of him sometime soon, he would be gone forever.

She finally slipped down, placing her feet on the floor, still holding his shoulders.

"It'll be better next time," he said. "We'll take a long time. You'll see." He leaned down to brush kisses on her mouth, her throat.

"It was perfect this time," she whispered before turning away to gather her clothes.

His fingers closed over her wrist. "Come on. I'll show you where a shower is."

He took her down a hall and into a spacious bedroom with polished oak flooring, a sofa, a desk, a big-screen television and a king-size bed. There was a big wooden rocker in the room along with a full-length mirror.

"Right through there is a shower and there should be fresh towels for you. I'm just across the hall."

She nodded and watched him as he left.

Would he disappear out of her life again soon? She intended to see that he didn't.

She showered, washed and dried her hair, and wrapping herself in a thick, pink towel, she went to find her clothes. When she opened the door and stepped into the hall, the bag she had brought from the ranch was waiting outside the door. Smiling, with a glance at the closed door across the hall, she gathered her things and went back inside, closing the door.

Shortly she was dressed in red slacks and a red short-sleeved shirt with flip-flops on her feet. She let her hair fall freely across her shoulders.

She left to find Jake, discovering him in the kitchen. She walked into the room with a high-beamed ceiling, a copper pot rack hanging over the center island workstation, cherry cabinets and stainless-steel appliances, making for a far more up-to-date kitchen than the one on the Milan ranch.

Jake had his back to her while he placed twice-baked potato halves to warm in the oven. He turned and stopped, his gaze roaming over her appreciatively and making her want to be in his arms again.

He crossed the kitchen to her and rested his hands on her hips. "You look too composed and refreshed. We may end up right back in bed."

"I'm not going to argue with that," she said, wrapping her arms around his neck, standing on tiptoe to brush his lips with hers.

His arm tightened around her waist, pulling her tightly

against him while he captured her mouth. With a pounding heart, she kissed him as if they hadn't just made love.

Finally he released her. "I'm fascinated with the old coins," he said.

"The coins are exciting." She didn't add that they weren't as exciting to her as he was.

She could swear his eyes were almost twinkling, and he looked like a kid at Christmas when he asked, "Want to go count them now?"

Seeing his excitement, she agreed.

"There's no way to know which family the gold belonged to," she said, following him into the family room. Jake set his drink on a table, hunkering down to tilt the metal box to dump out the coins.

She sat on the floor across from him and gold coins spilled out, sliding and building into a stack until some came to rest on her crossed feet. She could see inside the open chest and there was a small metal box in the bottom. She reached inside to take it out. "Jake, look. Here's something else," she said, raising the lid to see a folded paper inside.

She picked it up.

"Maddie, let me see that," he said, but she had already started unfolding it with great care.

Ten

"Maddie—" Jake said, stretching out his arm to take the paper from her, but she twisted out of his reach as she began to read.

"'To whom it may concern. Having just lost in a game of chance with cards, a gambling game, I hereby pay in gold one half of my debt to Reuben Calhoun.'" Her mouth went dry and her heart began to pound, but she continued with the note.

"'For the other part of my debt I deed a ten-acre strip of land from the west boundary to the east boundary, along the entire north side of my property, to Reuben Calhoun.' It's signed 'Mortimer Milan.'"

"Maddie, wait a minute—" Jake ordered.

Hurting again as she had so long ago by his actions, she turned to look at him. "This is a deed for part of our ranch to go to the Calhouns. There are witnesses. It's dated 1887." She stared at him while pain squeezed her heart.

"You were after this deed all along. That's why you said I could have the gold if we found it."

Angry, feeling betrayed all over again, she stood and flung the ancient paper at him. "Answer me. You knew about this deed, didn't you?"

"Listen to me." He stood facing her. "Yes, I knew about it."

Closing her eyes, she rocked on her heels as if he had physically hit her, only the blow was to her heart.

"Maddie, I don't want it now."

She opened her eyes. "I don't believe you. You set this all up to see if you could find the deed and have that much of our ranch because that's where you want to drill.

"Don't lie to me, Jake," she demanded, her face flushing. "That's why you wanted to look for the treasure, not for your ancestors' remains. Answer me. That's why you got into this search, isn't it?"

"Yes, it was in the beginning because we were still angry with each other. Maddie," he said, walking around the gold between them.

She was shaking as she faced him and she stepped back to avoid his touch. "Take the property. You succeeded completely and you've made a fool of me in doing so."

Closing the distance, he grasped her shoulders and held her. "Listen to me. I don't want it. I wouldn't think of hurting you that way. Not now."

"I don't believe you," she said, his deceit turning her to ice.

He leaned down and caught up the letter and the deed that was rolled up, tied with a strip of leather with writing on the outside of it.

He handed her the deed. "This may be the real thing and the only copy. Who knows. I'm sure it's the first deed to this land." He held up the letter and tore it in two.

Stunned, Madison watched him. "What are you doing?"

"I would never hurt you deliberately."

"Your family knew you were doing this in hopes of finding the deed, didn't they? They'll expect that land to go to them."

He caught her wrist and picked up the two pieces of the letter. "Come here," he said, taking her into the kitchen. Still shocked by his tearing up the letter, she followed and watched as he opened a drawer to get a box of matches, striking one. Standing over the sink, he set fire to the lower part of the two strips of paper. He glanced at her as the paper burned brightly.

She could only stare at the flames engulfing the letter as it swiftly disappeared. He dropped the remains into the sink before they burned his hand and she watched them curl into black cinders with a plume of fading gray smoke.

"There is no evidence of any change in the Milan deed now," he said.

Momentarily speechless, she stared at him. "Why?" she whispered, unable to get the word out clearly. She gulped for breath. "You did all that searching for the treasure just to get that letter."

Jake stared at her, his own thoughts in turmoil. "I love you," he said, declaring it as if more to himself than her. "Maddie, I just realized that I'm in love with you," he said. He stepped closer to take her in his arms. He felt dazed, but he couldn't bear to hurt her and he realized he did not want to lose her a second time.

"I promise you, I will not take your property and neither will my family. First of all the letter has been destroyed, so now no one can use it. Second—I wouldn't let them take your property if they tried. Third—no living person knows about that letter except the two of us."

"Your family will ask you. Tell them the truth, Jake."

"They'll understand why and if any of them don't, so be

it. If we get into it about the land, I can pay them for their share. I don't care. I love you with all my heart. Maybe I always have deep down. There's really never been any other woman I've been deeply interested in since high school. I love you," he declared again.

Would she accept what he was telling her? He hoped he'd proved his feelings for her. Hoped she realized that to do what he had just done, he had to love her deeply.

He searched her eyes for a clue to her feelings, and saw all the hurt vanish faster than the letter had, replaced by a shimmering glow. Tears spilled down her cheeks as she reached for him, and he gasped for the breath he'd been holding.

"Oh, Jake," she said, "I love you with all my heart. I thought I was losing you again. And I misjudged you again—I'm sorry."

"Shh, Maddie. Originally, I was searching for that deed to wave it in your dad's face. Sorry." Jake pulled her into his embrace, wrapping his arms around her while he lowered his head to kiss her.

In minutes he picked her up, carrying her to his bedroom, yanking back the covers on the bed and then pulling her into his arms to kiss her again. He had a lot to prove to her, yet again.

Later, Madison lay beside Jake with his arm around her. She shifted and turned to look at him and he rolled on his side to face her. "What?" he said.

"Won't your family be terribly unhappy with you?"

"For burning the letter? I don't think so. We're all well-fixed. We don't need to take part of your land. You've told me I can lease a piece of your land or present you with an offer and you'll listen."

"Yes, but you'll be paying the Milans for the lease.

That's different from you owning the land," she said, thinking about what he had just said to her.

He propped his head on his hand to look at her. "I love you, Maddie. I've been searching my feelings, but when you got so angry, I was afraid I was going to lose you again. I don't want that to happen. I want you in my life all the time. This week has been the best week of my life since I was a teenager. The love we had then has gone because it was different. We were kids and I'll have to admit, maybe your dad was right about us being too young to marry. He just went about keeping us apart in a terrible way."

"I know he did, Jake. I have never known that side of my dad. I didn't dream he was capable of doing something so hurtful."

"It's over. We've got now," he said, hugging her and shifting so he could kiss her.

"Maddie, I heard an 'I love you' from you earlier tonight, didn't I?"

She raised her head and met his gaze, and now she wasn't afraid to admit it. "Yes, you did, because I do. I've realized that I love you."

"I love you, too," he said, hugging her. He leaned back and propped his head up. "I want to take you out tomorrow night. We haven't had a fair chance with all that's been happening. Will you go to dinner with me tomorrow night?"

"I would love to go to dinner with you," she said, smiling at him.

"Perfect. We need a fun night out."

She snuggled against him, feeling as if her life was back on an even keel and good once more, finally. In her mind she could hear Jake saying "I love you" again and again.

Thursday night she stood in front of her mirror, checking herself over far too many times to keep track. She wanted to look her best for Jake. He had seen her in her jeans and cutoffs, out hunting treasure all day with him.

She was dressed in a red sleeveless dress with her hair falling free the way he liked it. She had diamond stud earrings in her ears and high-heeled red pumps that matched her knee-length dress. She was eager to be with him, and when she heard the door chimes, she flew to the door.

Smiling, she opened the door to face him and her breath caught in her throat.

Dressed in a navy suit with a white shirt and red tie, he looked more handsome than ever before. His gaze ran over her and the warm approval showed in his dark brown eyes. "You're gorgeous," he said in a husky tone.

"Thank you. Come in and I'll get my purse," she said, stepping back. He entered and waited quietly while she picked up her red purse and joined him.

As they rode in the limo to the airport, he held her hand. "This is the first chance I've had to tell you—I've talked to my siblings about the gold and invited them out Saturday night for a cookout. The gold is still in my vault at the ranch, so I'll show them my share."

It wasn't so much the gold that had her worried. "Have you told them about the deed?"

"Yes, and nobody raised an objection. They're okay with the whole deal."

"I can't imagine. Especially your sister."

"Lindsay surprised me a little because she was willing to accept whatever I decided."

"That's great," Madison said, unable to imagine Lindsay Calhoun yielding so gracefully to her brother's wishes where it involved a Milan.

"I've thought about it and I'll be happy to invite your family, too, on Saturday if they want to come."

"My brothers are fascinated and amazed that we found the treasure."

"I still am. I never really expected to find anything."

"I didn't, either."

"Maddie, there's something else. While I was at my office today, your dad called me. He said he wants to talk to me. He asked for an appointment to come to my office, so we have one tomorrow afternoon at four."

"I hope he apologizes, although he can't really undo what he's done," she said, looking at Jake and wanting to kiss him. She couldn't get enough of him and now that they had both said they were in love, her feelings for him seemed to strengthen steadily. She reached out to hold his hand. He smiled, giving her hand a light squeeze.

"I'll let you know about your dad. Now enough about the family. Let's think about us. Although if I think about you too much, we may have to cut short this evening by quite a bit."

Laughing, she hugged him. She felt giddy with love for him.

They flew in his jet to Dallas, where they went to an elegant new restaurant on the twenty-fifth floor where the view overlooked the city. Jake ordered wine for them, and after it had been tasted, approved and poured, he asked her to dance.

She stepped into his arms and was carried back to high school, to being young, carefree and so in love with him. She looked up at him, smiling, winding her arms around his neck.

"This is good, Jake. I didn't expect to ever be dancing with you again."

"I agree. It's very good."

They danced a slow number, next a fast dance and returned to their table. They sipped their wine and he gazed at her over candlelight. "How did it go when you took in the gold?"

She smiled. "You know who did it. Wyatt came in his

sheriff's car to take it to the bank. Nick and Tony were with him and they all had to see the coins. I told them each to take ten home for now. They were amazed that the coins really existed, but none of us knows who the Milan was who was named Mortimer. Some of our property goes back that far, but the Double M was named for Michael Milan."

"Did you tell any of them about the letter and the deed?"

"Yes and they're all three shocked that you burned the letter. They were impressed by your generosity, that's for certain, and maybe that made a dent in the old feud. At least for Wyatt and Nick. My brothers are really surprised to find the treasure actually existed, as well as the deed, and I think they're as fascinated by the coins as I am. Now the coins are deposited safely in the Bank of Verity," she said, smiling at him.

"Good place for them to be."

When the small band started the next song, she recognized the ballad as the one they called "our song" when they had been in high school.

Still in his arms out on the dance floor, she looked up at him. "Did you ask them to play that song?"

Jake smiled. "Yes. I wanted to see if you remembered."

"I remember so much," she said. "That was a special time in our lives." She danced with him, holding him close as joy bubbled inside because she was in his arms and he seemed as happy as she.

Later, after dinner, he took her to his house in a gated area in a new suburban section, set back on a landscaped lawn. Her gaze roamed over the two-story Colonial that was large but not the mansion she guessed he would have. Inside he showed her the downstairs, after which they sat in the large family room, where he stepped behind the bar to pour nightcaps and then returned to sit with her on a dark brown leather couch.

He shed his coat and tie, unbuttoning the top buttons of

his shirt while she watched him. "Keep going," she said when he stopped, and he grinned at her as he took her drink from her hand and set it on a glass coffee table. He reached into his pocket and sat beside her.

"Maddie, will you marry me?"

As her heart thudded, she flung her arms around his neck. "I love you, Jake. Of course I'll marry you," she cried, joy bringing tears of happiness to her eyes.

He leaned back. "Hey, don't start crying."

"I'm so happy," she said, watching as he took her hand and slipped the ring on her finger.

"I love you and I'll try to always make you happy," he said.

"Jake, this is beautiful," she said, looking at the large diamond, surrounded by an intricate design of smaller diamonds. "This is just gorgeous. And it fits." She looked up at him and could see the love she felt mirrored in his eyes. She threw her arms around him to hug him while she kissed him.

In a few moments he paused to face her again. "I should tell your dad, and I will, but there's no way I'm asking for his permission."

She laughed. "No, you're not. You don't even have to tell him. I will. Some of the Milans and Calhouns are going to have to start speaking to each other now that they will be in-laws."

He grinned. "They'll adjust. I don't care what they do, really. I love you and that's all that really matters to me. And please, my big request is let's not wait forever for a wedding."

"Suits me fine," she answered, looking at her ring. "Jake, this is the most beautiful ring I've ever seen."

"You might be exaggerating there, but I'm glad you're happy with it. Ahh, I love you, darlin'. With all my heart, forever." He drew her into his embrace again and kissed away her reply. Finally, she looked up at him.

"Jake, we're going to have to tell our families. I'm too excited to wait even though it's kind of late. Tony is just going to have to adjust to having a Calhoun for a brother-in-law."

"I don't know whether he can stop fighting with Lindsay long enough to try to be friends. And I will have a talk with Lindsay about her attitude. Mike's another one."

"We should call your parents first. I barely know them."

"Doesn't matter. Everyone can get to know each other. We're the ones getting married and that's all that's really important. They should act civil to each other through the wedding."

She laughed. "I can't stop laughing. I feel giddy with happiness. Get your phone and let's start calling. I'm telling Tony first and then Wyatt and Nick if we can find him."

Jake picked her up and placed her in his lap, holding her and smiling at her. "This is going to be so good, Maddie. We have a lot of years to make up for."

She felt a warm glow of joy as she wrapped her arms around his neck and smiled in return. "You're going to have to put up with my art and with me traveling to New Mexico, though for much shorter trips than I'm used to. For now, I'd like to keep the gallery I have there. It helps that I have good people running it."

"Sure, just like you'll have to put up with my traveling. I promise you, though, I've always had a schedule and I intend to retire from that business in about ten more years to be a rancher all the time. This is what I love."

"We'll work it all out." She held his jaw to get his full attention. "Jake, we've lost a lot of years together. I want your babies, a family. Soon. How do you feel about it?"

He smiled at her and leaned forward to kiss her lightly.

"I think that's great. We both grew up in families with several kids. That's what I want, too, Maddie."

They kissed, long and deeply, a kiss that to her was a promise and a physical bonding that reflected the feelings in her heart. When she leaned away, she looked up.

"I love you more than I can ever tell you or show you. It'll take a lifetime."

"I feel the same way, and right now, I feel like the luckiest man on the planet."

She laughed. "That's an exaggeration, but I'm glad you feel that way. This is wonderful, Jake, and no one will stop us or interfere this time. This wedding will set a record for how fast it gets planned."

"They sure won't stop us and fast is great."

"Jake, I'm going to become a Calhoun. Mercy!"

He grinned, kissing her cheek. "You will be the most beautiful Calhoun to ever be in the family. You'll be a good influence on the Calhouns for sure, and maybe this may be the death knell for the feud."

She sat up and reached for her phone. "I'm calling Tony."

"I'm going to ask your brothers to be groomsmen."

"That's nice, Jake. Then I should ask Lindsay to be a bridesmaid, but I think she'll turn me down." She shook her finger at him. "And don't you browbeat her into accepting."

"Fine," he agreed, feigning a sheepish face. "Whatever you want. Just as long as you pick a date tonight before we call everyone." He found the calendar on his phone.

"We could have a Christmas wedding."

Jake groaned. "You're not listening to me. I said you couldn't make me wait. How about a September wedding?"

"This month?" She laughed. "That's impossible."

"Are we going to have our first fight?"

"Absolutely not. I promise very soon—I'll aim for setting a record for planning a big wedding."

"I'm anxious. I can't wait. Ahh, darlin', I've waited too long in the past. I can pay for the wedding and I can afford to pay rush rates."

"You don't have to pay for the wedding. Dad owes us this. And we will have a rush job. But a deluxe one," she said.

Jake grinned and shook his head. "Why do I think this wedding is going to cost the judge a small fortune?"

"I meant it when I said Dad owes us. Think of the biggest church in Dallas and let's rent the whole country club for the reception. If we can't get it on short notice, we'll go elsewhere."

"Maddie, let it go. We don't need a whole country club," he said, chuckling.

She studied the calendar. "Okay, this is almost humanly impossible for a big wedding, but we can do it if we pay extra for services. How about the first Saturday morning in October?"

"Ahh, that's my darlin'. I'd prefer this weekend, but the first Saturday in October isn't bad. Do you have any druthers for a honeymoon?"

"Only with you," she said, smiling.

"Great. Now for the phone calls. We have a wedding to plan."

"An expensive wedding," she added, laughing with him.

Epilogue

Madison stood with her arm linked through her father's as they stood in the vestibule of the church. She could see Jake, tall and handsome, waiting for her at the altar. The men in the Milan and Calhoun families were handsome. Her gaze ran down the line of eight groomsmen, which included her brothers as well as Jake's.

The problem person had been Lindsay, who had coolly and politely turned down Madison's invitation to be a bridesmaid. Jake had insisted there were no hard feelings over her rejection, but Madison wondered. She suspected Lindsay would not speak to her tonight, because she usually didn't speak if they encountered each other in Verity.

Madison didn't want a hostile bridal attendant, even if she was her future sister-in-law, so she was not unhappy to have Lindsay turn her down. The bridesmaids were all her friends plus a cousin and a relative Madison had always been close friends with.

Jake had the same sort of arrangement because he had a cousin as a groomsman. Friends and cousins served as ushers for Jake and she had friends and cousins who would be at the guest register.

Her father squeezed her hand, getting her attention. "Madison, I know I've told you this a hundred times, but I'll tell you one last time—I'm sorry you and Jake were hurt," her father said. "I wish you all the happiness possible now."

"Thank you," she said, gazing into his blue eyes and knowing it was time to accept his apology and forgive him. Glancing at Jake, her thoughts changed to when they could get away from their reception for their honeymoon.

Soon the bridesmaids began their walk down the aisle. With a fanfare of trumpets, violins started the wedding march as the wedding planner cued Madison and her father to walk down the aisle.

Her gaze flew to Jake's and she never saw anyone else while she walked slowly beside her dad. With each step her happiness grew. She would finally marry Jake. It seemed right and so long awaited.

When his dark brown eyes met her gaze, she was eager to repeat her vows and become Mrs. Jacob Calhoun.

Finally they reached the altar and Jake came forward. She didn't even hear her father's reply when he released her hand and Jake's fingers wrapped around hers as he stepped to her side. He looked down at her and smiled, enveloping them both in their own world on the best day of her life.

They repeated vows, prayed, listened to solos and finally they were introduced to the guests as Mr. and

Mrs. Jacob Calhoun. To her delight, she had just become Jake's wife.

They rushed back up the aisle and out to go around and come back for pictures.

In an empty hallway Jake halted to draw her into his arms. "I love you, Mrs. Calhoun."

She smiled at him. "I hope you do half as much as I love you."

He kissed her hard, possessively, and she returned his kiss, looking forward to their wedding night and every night thereafter.

The reception was at the country club. The train to her white satin designer dress had been removed, leaving her in a strapless sheath. Her hair was swept in an updo, and she had already shed her veil.

The crowd spilled outside onto the veranda. It was a sunny, warm fall day in Dallas and children of guests played on the lawn.

All afternoon while she talked to guests, Madison was aware of Jake in various parts of the room or out on the terrace.

Occasionally, she would lose sight of him, but then she would spot him again.

It was late afternoon and she was talking with some friends when Jake walked up to take her arm. "If you ladies will excuse us, someone wants to see Madison."

They moved away and he headed toward the kitchen door.

"Where are we going and who wants to see me?" she asked, smiling to friends as she passed them.

"I want to see you in the worst way and we are going to a waiting limousine. Your maid of honor, Carol, is waiting in the kitchen to get your bouquet to toss it in your place if you can forgo the thrill of throwing your bouquet."

She laughed. "I can, but now Carol doesn't have a chance to catch it."

"I believe the lady is already wearing an engagement ring on her finger, so I don't think she needs to catch the bouquet. Are you arguing about leaving with me now?"

"Not one word," she said, grasping his hand and moving ahead of him. They entered the kitchen while the staff smiled and waved to her. If she passed close to any of them, she thanked them for their help.

Jake held the door and they stepped to the delivery drive behind the kitchen. A high fence surrounded the area with thick shrubbery along the fence to hide the back door.

A sleek black limo waited and a chauffeur held the door for them, closing it behind them once they got in. In seconds he pulled the limo away.

Turning to her, Jake took her into his arms. "Mrs. Calhoun, how I've waited for you to be my bride." He kissed her, a long kiss that she wanted to never end.

His jet waited and by nightfall they were in a penthouse in New York. She briefly saw the balcony and the city lights, but then she was in Jake's arms and the world was forgotten.

She pushed the jacket to his tux off his shoulders and tossed it onto a chair. In the plane she had changed from her wedding gown to a knee-length pale blue silk dress. Jake's fingers moved deftly at the back of her neck and she felt cool air as he pulled the zipper down slowly and then pushed the dress away. He held her away from him so he could look at her for moments.

"You're beautiful, Maddie. I love you more every day."

She stepped into his arms and stood on tiptoe to kiss him, holding him tightly. Jake leaned over her, wrapping his arms tightly around her. "I love you, darlin', with all my heart."

Joyously, she kissed him, certain this tall, handsome Texas rancher was the love of her life and always had been.

* * * * *

If you loved this LONE STAR LEGENDS *story,
pick up* USA TODAY *bestselling author
Sara Orwig's other Western-set series:*

STETSONS & CEOS

*DAKOTA DADDY
MONTANA MISTRESS
WYOMING WEDDING
TEXAS TYCOON'S CHRISTMAS FIANCÉE
TEXAS-SIZED TEMPTATION
A LONE STAR LOVE AFFAIR
WILD WESTERN NIGHTS*

and

LONE STAR LEGACY

*RELENTLESS PURSUIT
THE RELUCTANT HEIRESS
MIDNIGHT UNDER THE MISTLETOE
ONE TEXAS NIGHT...
HER TEXAN TO TAME*

All available now from Harlequin Desire!

REQUEST YOUR FREE BOOKS!
2 FREE NOVELS PLUS 2 FREE GIFTS!

ALWAYS POWERFUL, PASSIONATE AND PROVOCATIVE

YES! Please send me 2 FREE Harlequin Desire® novels and my 2 FREE gifts (gifts are worth about $10). After receiving them, if I don't wish to receive any more books, I can return the shipping statement marked "cancel." If I don't cancel, I will receive 6 brand-new novels every month and be billed just $4.55 per book in the U.S. or $4.99 per book in Canada. That's a savings of at least 13% off the cover price! It's quite a bargain! Shipping and handling is just 50¢ per book in the U.S. and 75¢ per book in Canada.* I understand that accepting the 2 free books and gifts places me under no obligation to buy anything. I can always return a shipment and cancel at any time. Even if I never buy another book, the two free books and gifts are mine to keep forever.

225/326 HDN F4ZC

Name	(PLEASE PRINT)	
Address		Apt. #
City	State/Prov.	Zip/Postal Code

Signature (if under 18, a parent or guardian must sign)

Mail to the **Harlequin® Reader Service:**
IN U.S.A.: P.O. Box 1867, Buffalo, NY 14240-1867
IN CANADA: P.O. Box 609, Fort Erie, Ontario L2A 5X3

Want to try two free books from another line?
Call 1-800-873-8635 or visit www.ReaderService.com.

* Terms and prices subject to change without notice. Prices do not include applicable taxes. Sales tax applicable in N.Y. Canadian residents will be charged applicable taxes. Offer not valid in Quebec. This offer is limited to one order per household. Not valid for current subscribers to Harlequin Desire books. All orders subject to credit approval. Credit or debit balances in a customer's account(s) may be offset by any other outstanding balance owed by or to the customer. Please allow 4 to 6 weeks for delivery. Offer available while quantities last.

Your Privacy—The Harlequin® Reader Service is committed to protecting your privacy. Our Privacy Policy is available online at www.ReaderService.com or upon request from the Harlequin Reader Service.

We make a portion of our mailing list available to reputable third parties that offer products we believe may interest you. If you prefer that we not exchange your name with third parties, or if you wish to clarify or modify your communication preferences, please visit us at www.ReaderService.com/consumerschoice or write to us at Harlequin Reader Service Preference Service, P.O. Box 9062, Buffalo, NY 14269. Include your complete name and address.

HDI3R

SPECIAL EXCERPT FROM

 HARLEQUIN

Desire

Turn the page for a sneak peek at USA TODAY
bestselling author **Kathie DeNosky**'s

LURED BY THE RICH RANCHER, the fourth novel in
Harlequin Desire's **DYNASTIES: THE LASSITERS** *series.*

*It's city vs. country when Chance Lassiter meets
PR exec Felicity Sinclair....*

"**W**ould you like to dance, Ms. Sinclair?"

She glanced at her uncomfortable-looking high heels.
"I...hadn't thought I would be dancing."

Laughing, Chance Lassiter bent down to whisper close
to her ear. "I'm from the school of stand in one place and
sway."

Her delightful laughter caused a warm feeling to spread
throughout his chest. "I think that's about all I'll be able to
do in these shoes anyway."

When she placed her soft hand in his and stood up to walk
out onto the dance floor with him, an electric current shot
straight up his arm. He wrapped his arms loosely around her
and smiled down at her upturned face.

"Chance, there's something I'd like to discuss with you,"
she said as they swayed back and forth.

"I'm all ears," he said, grinning.

"I'd like your help with my public relations campaign to
improve the Lassiters' image."

"Sure. I'll do whatever I can to help you out," he said,
drawing her a little closer. "What did you have in mind?"

"You're going to be the family spokesman for the PR campaign that I'm planning," she said, beaming.

Marveling at how beautiful she was, it took a moment for her words to register with him. He stopped swaying and stared down at her in disbelief. "You want me to do what?"

"I'm going to have you appear in all future advertising for Lassiter Media," she said, sounding extremely excited. "You'll be in the national television commercials, as well as…"

Chance silently ran through every cuss word he'd ever heard. He might be a Lassiter, but he wasn't as refined as the rest of the family. Instead of riding a desk in some corporate office, he was on the back of a horse every day herding cattle under the wide Wyoming sky. That was the way he liked it and the way he intended for things to stay. There was no way in hell he was going to be the family spokesman. And the sooner he could find a way to get that across to her, the better.

Don't miss
LURED BY THE RICH RANCHER
by Kathie DeNosky.

Available July 2014,
wherever Harlequin® Desire books are sold.